BILL NYE the Science Guy's®

GREAT BIG BOOK OF SCIENCE

featuring

OCEANS AND DINOSAURS

With additional writing by
Ian G. Saunders

Illustrated by
John S. Dykes and Michael Koelsch

Hyperion Paperbacks for Children • New York

BILL NYE the Science Guy's® BIG BLUE OCEAN

Printed in Singapore
Book design by Angela Corbo Gier
Cover design by Elizabeth Clark
First compiled edition, 2005
1 3 5 7 9 10 8 6 4 2
Library of Congress Cataloging-in-Publication Data on file.
ISBN 0-7868-5591-6 (compiled pbk. edition)

Visit www.hyperionbooksforchildren.com

All Bill Nye photos by Rex Rystedt; pp. 8–10 border © 1999 by Joshua Singer; p. 9: coelocanth © 1999 by Mark V. Erdmann; mudskipper © 1999 by Sunset (Brake)/Peter Arnold, Inc.; eel © 1995 by Gail Shumway/FPG International LLC; guitarfish © 1999 by Marilyn Kazmers/Peter Arnold, Inc.; p. 10: all fish on bottom © 1999 by Joshua Singer; pp. 12–14 border © 1999 by Jeffry W. Meyers/FPG International LLC; p. 14: evisceration © 1999 by Mark V. Erdmann; p. 22: border © 1999 by Joshua Singer; p. 48: border by Rex Rysted. Library of Congress Cataloging-in-Publication data on file. ISBN 0-7868-4221-0 (trade ed.) ISBN 0-7868-5063-9 (lib.ed.)

Part of the Big Blue Ocean is for my parents; they took me to the ocean often. Part is for Nathaniel Bowditch; he knew the science of the sea. Often I've stood on shore or on deck and wondered what all those Earthlings are doing there; here's hoping you do too. —B.N.

To my wife, Alissa Kozuh, for her loving and boundless support —I.S.

For Mom, Dad, Patti, Jeffrey, and Gregory —J.S.D.

CONTENTS

Introducing the BIG, Wide Ocean!

Next time you're in outer space, look down at your home planet. Or just look at a picture of Earth from space . . . it's blue. It's mostly ocean—liquid water—71 percent of our planet's surface is part of an ocean. And it's the ocean that keeps our planet full of life. All the other planets in our Solar System are either too far from or too close to the Sun to have oceans like ours.

Ocean water evaporates and becomes almost all the rain that falls everywhere on Earth. That's what lets plants and animals grow. Without the ocean, ours would be a bare, and probably lifeless, world.

The Seven Seas. You may have heard the expression "the Seven Seas," but that's really from a different time, before people had sailed all the way around the world. All of the oceans are connected. So if you look at the world one way, there's just one ocean. If you look at it another way, you could say there are four: the Pacific, the Atlantic, the Indian, and the Arctic Oceans.

The water in the ocean is the same water that Cleopatra sailed and that dinosaurs drank. It's the same water that filled the first cavepeople's swimming pool! Water in the ocean today is the same water that's been on Earth since the ocean was formed over 4 billion years ago.

It's a Big Secret. We can explore the deepest reaches of outer space—places millions of kilometers away—with a telescope from our backyard. But exploring the ocean is much more difficult. We need special equipment that can handle enormous pressures and corrosive chemicals. That's why the sea still holds most of its secrets.

The Ocean Is the Most Populated Place on Earth

Up high and shallow, or down low and deep, everywhere you go in the ocean you find living things. And fish aren't the only things out there. Birds (like penguins), reptiles (like sea turtles), mammals (like whales), not to mention tons of animals without backbones, called "invertebrates" [in-VERT-uh-brits] (like squid), and tons and tons of plants (like seaweed) all depend on the ocean to survive.

If you could weigh all the living things in the ocean and all the living things on land, the ocean life would weigh a thousand times as much as the living things on land. Look around and imagine a thousand times more life. For every person, tree, and mosquito you see, think of a thousand more. The ocean is where most earthlings live.

An Ocean Desert. The moving water of the ocean makes some parts of the ocean have way more life than others. There are "deserts" in the sea, like ones found off the coast of Chile, in South America, where there are relatively few living things. Other places in the ocean, like Australia's Great Barrier Reef, have more living things on and over every patch of sea floor than on and over every patch of ground in a tropical rain forest.

TRY THIS!

THE QUESTION:
How much of the Earth's surface is covered with water?

HERE'S WHAT YOU NEED:
a basketball • a roll of 2.5-cm-wide (1 inch) masking tape (preferably blue) • a friend

1. Find a basketball and a roll of masking tape. Blue masking tape might remind you of the blue ocean.
2. Measure out 517 centimeters (203 inches) of tape. It's pretty long. You can tear it any way you like as you measure.
3. Now stick the tape on the basketball without letting it overlap anywhere. You've covered the ball with as much tape as the Earth is covered with water. Try playing catch without touching the tape. We live on a very wet world.

That's a lot of water compared to land on Earth, isn't it?

What Makes a Fish a Fish?

Like us humans, fish have skeletons, complete with a backbone. Other sea creatures, like crabs and shrimp, have no backbone, so we don't call them fish. Unlike you, fish have gills to breathe underwater. Next time you're wondering if something's a fish, use this. . . .

HANDY FISH-OR-NOT CHECKLIST OF SCIENCE:

YES	NO	
✔	☐	Does he or she have a backbone?
✔	☐	Does he or she have gills?

If it's yes to both questions, then you're looking at a fish. (Unless it's an amphibian. For example, tadpoles start out with gills. Then they become frogs and grow arms, legs, and lungs.)

Smart Fish. Sometimes fish hang out together. Tuna swim together in groups of about twenty. Herring, another type of fish, travel in groups of hundreds of millions. We call a group of fish a "school." With all those fish watching out for each other and moving all the time, every fish in the school stands a better chance of surviving. See, schooling is smart for all kinds of species!

Been doin' the same thing down here for 65 million years.

The Living Fossil

In 1939, people fishing off the coast of South Africa caught a fish none of them had ever seen before. Two meters (6 feet) long and bright blue, with odd lumps on either side of its tail fin, the fish was a coelacanth [SEE-luh-kanth]. They were thought to have become extinct in the days of the dinosaurs. Since we now know where to look, scientists and curious fishermen have caught and photographed lots of coelacanths. In fact, so many have been caught now, that they may become an endangered species after hanging out on Earth for over 65 million years!

CHECK IT OUT!

Scientists have caught up with more than twenty thousand kinds of fish, and we figure there may be tens of thousands more swimming around out there. It would take more than a lifetime just to see one of every known type of fish living in the ocean.

more REAL LIFE fish tales

I can leave the ocean for hours and climb trees.

mudskipper

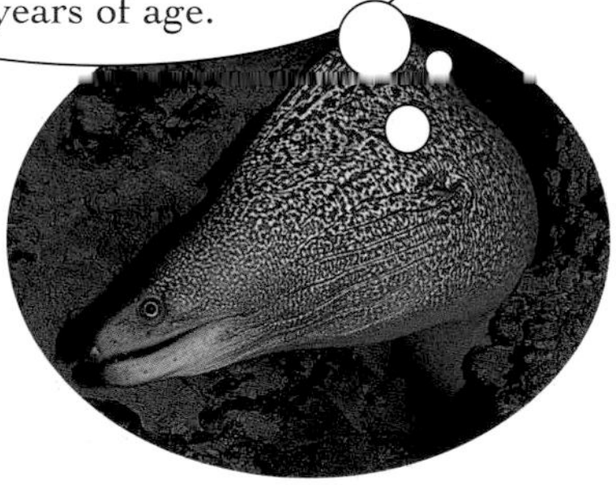

Some of us have lived to a ripe old eighty-eight years of age.

eel
(I'm another type of fish.)

guitarfish?
(nah . . . just kidding)

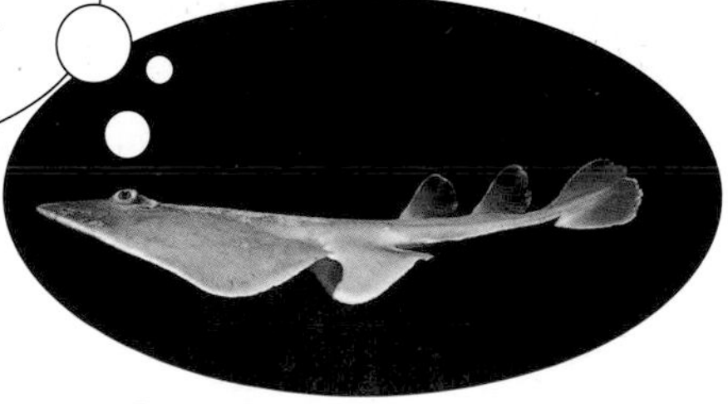

I have spines tipped with a venom as deadly as a rattlesnake's.

guitarfish (no kidding!)

Fish Can Drown! Humans can't breathe underwater. We use our lungs to get oxygen from the air we breathe, and the oxygen keeps us alive. Fish need oxygen, too. They get it out of the water using special organs called "gills." Each gill is a feathery membrane full of blood vessels. Gills move oxygen into a fish's blood the same way lungs move oxygen into our blood. Some gills are exposed, like a shark's. As a shark swims, water gets pumped through its gills. Other fish cover their gills with a hard plate called an operculum [oh-PERK-yoo-lum]. An operculum protects a fish's breathing apparatus.

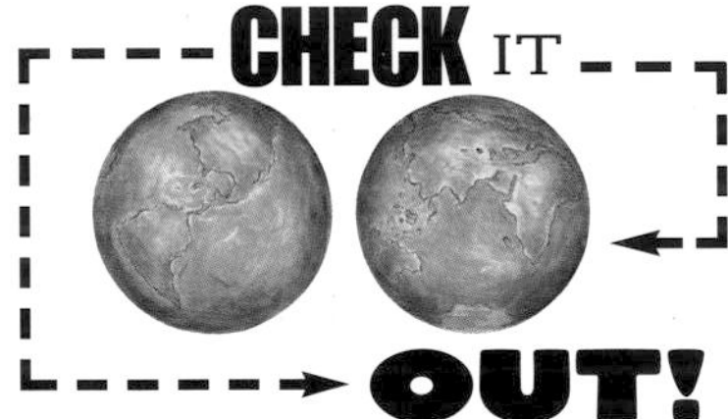

Just because fish have gills doesn't mean they don't need oxygen. If the water doesn't have enough oxygen in it, the fish can't survive. That's why fish tanks have pumps that bubble oxygen into the water.

All fish have gills. This includes the . . .

alligatorfish
birdfish
boarfish
buffalofish
catfish
crocodilefish
dogfish
elephantfish
frogfish
goatfish
goosefish
hawkfish
horsefish
lionfish
lizardfish
parrotfish
porcupinefish
rabbitfish
sheepfish
squirrelfish
tigerfish
toadfish
viperfish
wolffish
zebrafish

As you can see, there's a zoo full of gill-heads named after other animals. Some fish have even been named after other sea animals, like the whale shark. So far, we don't call any fish a fishfish. Hmm.

JUST TO SHOW A FEW

lionfish

crocodilefish

hawkfish

TRY THIS!

THE QUESTION:

How can we see the gases in water that fish need to breathe?

HERE'S WHAT YOU NEED:

an unopened bottle of soda • a balloon

1. Carefully fit a balloon all the way over a soda bottle that still has the cap on.
2. Keeping the balloon on with your fingers, unscrew the cap.

Bubbles of carbon dioxide gas will come out of the liquid and get captured by the balloon. Please note that there is more gas in a liter of soda than in a liter of seawater, because the soda bottle holds the soda under higher pressure than the atmosphere holds the surface of the sea.

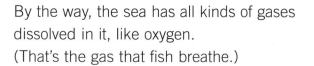

Gases can be dissolved in water. We can't see them, but fish can breathe them.

By the way, the sea has all kinds of gases dissolved in it, like oxygen. (That's the gas that fish breathe.)

SEA JELLIES

Animals Formerly Known as Jellyfish

Sea jellies are not fish. Remember, a fish has gills and a backbone. A sea jelly has gills, but no bones. Sea jellies are like round spoonfuls of jam. Of course, sometimes the spoonfuls are as big as manhole covers. They're mostly mesoglea **[MEZZ-uh-glee-uh]**—middle glue. Most sea jellies trail long, stinging tentacles below their bodies. Any animal that gets caught in the venomous sticky tentacles becomes lunch. A group of fish is called a "school"; a group of sea jellies is called a "smack."

animal + no backbone = invertebrate

Invertebrates. We call animals like sea jellies "invertebrates" [in-VERT-uh-brits], which means "no backbone." Other invertebrates, like octopuses (or octopi), squid, sea stars, sea pens, sea anemones, [uh-NEMM-uh-neez] and sea cucumbers, live all over in the ocean. Without bones or teeth, invertebrates have evolved special ways to survive in an ocean full of predators.

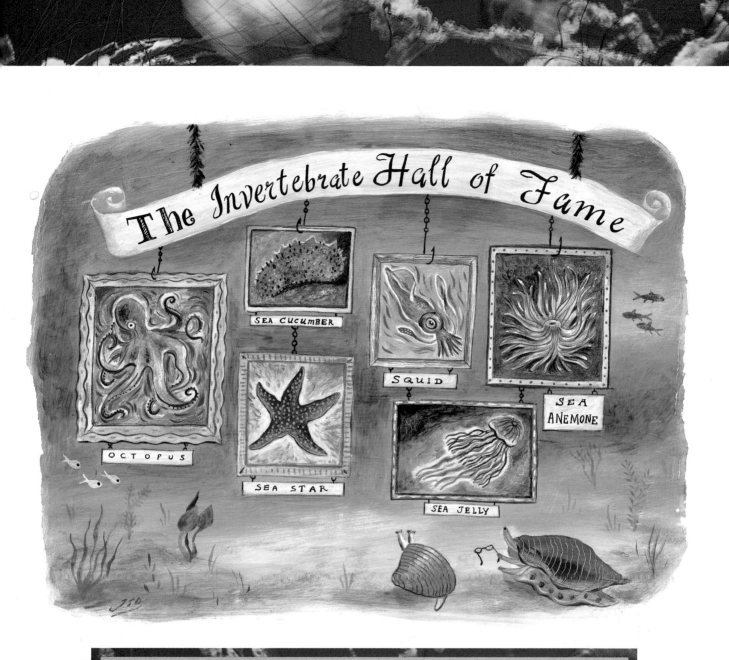

The Invertebrate Hall of Fame

SEA CUCUMBER
OCTOPUS
SQUID
SEA ANEMONE
SEA STAR
SEA JELLY

Invasion of the Head-foots. Squid and octopi are closely related to snails and clams. Even though they don't have a hard covering to protect themselves, they more than make up for it with muscular tentacles and deadly venoms. Plus, they can swim away from danger in a flash   well, in a cloud of ink. Long, thin squids squirt long, thin ink clouds. Short, wide ones squirt short, wide clouds. It's to fool a foe. Because their tentacles make up most of their body, and the rest of it is head, we call squid and octopi "cephalopods," [SEFF-uh-luh-Pahdz] a Greek word that means "head-foot."

When you see a sea star, it seems like it's sitting still, but sea stars really get around. We used to call sea stars "starfish." But they're not fish—no backbones. Some move at a rate of 10 centimeters (4 inches) a minute. Others travel about 3 nautical miles (3 1/2 miles) a month! Some sea stars team up in a big ball and roll along the bottom. When they smell a clam bed, the ball flies apart. The sea stars force clamshells open and eat the meat inside.

A sea cucumber feeds like a vacuum cleaner. To eat, they scoop up mud and lick tiny pieces of food off their finger-like tentacles. Sea cucumbers eat all the time. They can also spew their guts out to scare predators away. This behavior is called "evisceration" [eh-VISS-er-Ay-shun]. Sea cucumbers grow back new insides later on.

Evisceration in Action!

By the way, humans can't do this.

TRY THIS!

THE QUESTION:

How do squids defend themselves?

HERE'S WHAT YOU NEED:

handy squid reference of science • a clear bowl • water • food coloring

1. Draw a squid.
2. Fill a clear glass bowl with water.
3. Put your drawing underneath the bowl so you can see it through the water.
4. Now see how easy it is to squirt a cloud of food coloring that has the same shape.

It's not so easy, is it? But squids do it all the time.

Handy Squid Reference of Science

Be ready to dump the bowl out and start over. It's the kind of experiment that's perfect for your food preparation lab (your kitchen).

It's a Jungle Down There!

The ocean is like a jungle, where there are all kinds of food for all kinds of creatures. Mostly, large sea creatures eat smaller ones. For example, orcas eat seals. Seals, in turn, eat salmon. Salmon eat herring. Herring feed on the tiny plants and animals (plankton) that live near the surface of the ocean. We call this relationship a "food web." Each living thing in the web is connected to the other living things. There are millions of creatures that make up the huge, complex ocean food web.

There are vegetarian fish that eat plants. They're herbivores—plant eaters. Then there are fish that eat only meat, like the great white shark. They're carnivores. And there are even fish like us—that eat plants and other animals. We call these fish omnivores, which means "eats everything."

Surfing Tip of Science: Next time you hang ten, try not to look or splash like a seal. It may be that sometimes the silhouette of a surfer on a board looks like a tasty seal to a shark. Mmmmmm, yummy.

A Ferocious Hunter. The biggest carnivorous fish is the great white shark. It has several rows of sharp teeth that it uses to capture and tear into prey. Great whites usually attack from below. In the whole world, only about a dozen people die from shark attacks every year because sharks normally hunt ocean animals like seals, sea lions, or large fish.

Many fish find food by using their sense of smell. When scientists plugged the nostrils of catfish, the fish couldn't find food, even when they were looking right at it.

TRY THIS!

THE QUESTION:

How much stronger is a shark's sense of smell than a human's?

HERE'S WHAT YOU NEED:

microwave popcorn (or just a paper bag with unpopped corn kernels in it) • a gym with bleachers • a microwave an extension cord • a friend • a watch

1. Place a microwave in the middle of the gym and plug it in (you will probably need an extension cord to do this).
2. Have your friend sit down on the floor about 3 meters (10 feet) from the microwave.
3. Pop the popcorn.
4. Walk up to the last bleacher and sit down on it.
5. Time how long it takes for your friend to smell the popcorn.
6. Now time how long the smell takes to reach you.

Just think, a shark can smell from a hundred bleachers farther away than you can!

SEA PLANTS

Seaweed is not a weed. Certain sea plants are like sea trees growing together in a sea forest. They're big and beautiful. They're called kelp plants. Sometimes we call all kinds of sea plants "seaweed," probably because some kinds can tangle boat propellers and swimmers' arms. But they're not really weeds. They're lovely and vital. Ocean plants, like plants on land, convert sunlight and water into the oxygen that animals breathe. And ocean plants provide a rich source of food for all the creatures in the sea. Without sea plants, animals in the ocean would have nothing to breathe and nothing to eat.

You might have eaten some seaweed today and not even known it. Certain kinds of kelp are used in ice cream, candy bars, and salad dressing recipes.

Ahhhh... Seaweed isn't the only kind of plant in the ocean. There are quadrillions of tiny phytoplankton [FIE-tuh-plank-tun] drifting in the sea, too. They're like microscopic seaweed. These plants make so much oxygen that about a third of the oxygen you breathe probably comes from phytoplankton. Weird, huh?

Most Earthlings Eat Plankton

Plankton is what we call the mass of all the tiny plants and animals that live in the sea. They're usually too small to see with just our eyes. Plankton comes from the Greek word for "drifter" or "wanderer." Sometimes we use the word "plankter" for one animal or one plant that drifts as part of the plankton. And that's what members of the plankton do. They drift with the ocean's currents. More than 90 percent of living things in the sea are members of the plankton. Fish and other animals eat plankton. Then larger animals eat the smaller animals. Without plankton, just about every creature in the ocean food web would disappear.

ICE CREAM
All the animals that swim on their own are grouped together and called the "nekton" [NEK-tahn]—the swimmers. The creatures that live on the bottom are called the "benthon" [BENN-thahn].

Some whales have long plates in their mouths made of a special material called "baleen" [bay-LEEN], which feels like very thick fingernails. They use baleen plates like giant strainers, trapping small shrimp called krill and other plankters in their mouths while forcing seawater out with their tongues. By swimming and straining with its baleen plates, a whale eats tons of plankton. A blue whale is the largest animal on Earth. He or she consumes about 4 tons of krill every single day. That would be like eating 16,000 plates of spaghetti every 24 hours. Some scientists think that plankton will become a common source of food for humans in the twenty-first century. Whew!

In 1950, Thor Heyerdahl, a Norwegian explorer, sailed across the Pacific Ocean on a balsa-wood raft. Along the way, his crew trolled with a fine silk net. The net strained plankton from the sea, like a whale's baleen, and then the crew made soup with it. Someday, maybe you'll munch on a "McPlank" sandwich. Mmmm.

Plant Plankton

The phytoplankton are plants too small to see with just your eyes. Like miniature blades of grass, phtyoplankters live near the surface and soak up the Sun.

Animal Plankton

The zooplankton [ZOH-uh-plank-tun] are microscopic animals. They graze on phytoplankton and hunt each other.

TRY THIS!

THE QUESTION:

How much would a human have to eat if he/she was a whale?

HERE'S WHAT YOU NEED:

a scale • a typical lunch • peas

1 Take a scale. On one side, put everything that you would eat for lunch (for example, a peanut butter sandwich, a bag of pretzels, and an apple).
2 On the other side, pile up as many peas as it takes to balance out your meal.

If you were a whale, in a way, that's how much plankton you would have to eat to have lunch! If you can, try balancing everything you have to eat all day with peas.

Today the part of the plankton will be played by the peas.
PRETZELS
Peas of science

Reef Sweet Reef

A coral reef is made by tiny coral-making animals called polyps [PAHL-ips]. They take a mineral called calcium carbonate right out of the water and secrete it as a hard, protective, cup-shaped skeleton. We call the colonies of stuck together chalk cups coral reefs. The Great Barrier Reef, off the northeast coast of Australia, stretches 2,000 kilometers (1,250 miles). It's the largest coral structure on Earth. Sea urchins, sea stars, clams, crabs, and one-third of all the world's species of fish live in and around coral reefs.

At first, a coral reef doesn't seem to have many plants. But if you look closely, you'll find tiny plants, zooxanthellae [ZOH-uh-Zan-thell-ee], actually living in the tissues of the coral animals, the polyps. At night, the polyps use their tiny tentacles and stinging cells to capture zooplankton from the water around them just like tiny sea anemones. During the day, the polyps's tentacles contract and let the cells in their bodies with the zooxanthellae inside make food from sunlight. Coral reefs are built out of chalk dissolved in the sea by tiny animals with tiny plants living inside them!

The polyps, zooxanthellae, and skeletons are all needed to make a coral reef. It is a special ecosystem with a delicate balance of temperature, wave action, sunlight, and chemicals in the sea.

All the plankton in a coral reef typically weighs three times as much as the coral itself.

TRY THIS!

THE QUESTION:

How does sunlight affect coral reefs?

HERE'S WHAT YOU NEED:

seeds • a lamp • potting soil • 2 small flowerpots or empty film canisters • a lamp • a table • 2 or 3 books a plastic bag big enough to fit around the books • a shoe box

1 Plant seeds (I'm kooky for cabbage seeds!) in two separate little pots. Film canisters with good soil and a little water work great.

2 Place the plants under a light. Prop one up with books, on top of a table, so that it gets very close to the light. (If you put the books in a plastic bag, they won't get wet.) Put the other one on the floor on a shoebox, so that it's less likely to get kicked.

3 Water them now and then.

4 Watch them grow for a week or two.

The plant that is closer to the light will grow faster, just like the phytoplankton that corals depend on. The closer they grow to the sea's surface, the more light they get from the Sun. So the coral skeletons farther from the surface get abandoned as new coral animals grow above them.

The OCEAN Holds the Salt!

For billions of years, salt has washed into the ocean. When the Earth first formed, it was a mass of hot rock, like lava from a volcano. There were no living things, no video games, and no oceans. The Earth was probably completely covered with clouds. Any rain that fell on the ground would have heated up immediately and turned to steam. After millions of years, the surface of our planet cooled into a hard crust. The rains created the ocean. It probably rained for thousands of years without stopping. And as water ran downhill over the land, it carried bits of minerals with it, including salt. Once salt gets carried from land to the ocean, it's stuck. Salt's got nowhere else to go.

So Much Salt. On average, the ocean is 35 parts salt per 1,000 parts water. For every 1-liter soda bottle of seawater, there's $1\frac{1}{2}$ tablespoons (35 grams) of salt.

In places that don't get a lot of rain, like the Middle East, scientists have come up with ways to take the salt out of seawater. Sometimes we boil the seawater, and cool it back to a liquid. Water from vapor has no salt. Or we pump seawater through special membranes that hold salt back like a filter. Either way, we can "desalinate" [dee-SAL-in-ate] water from the ocean and drink it.

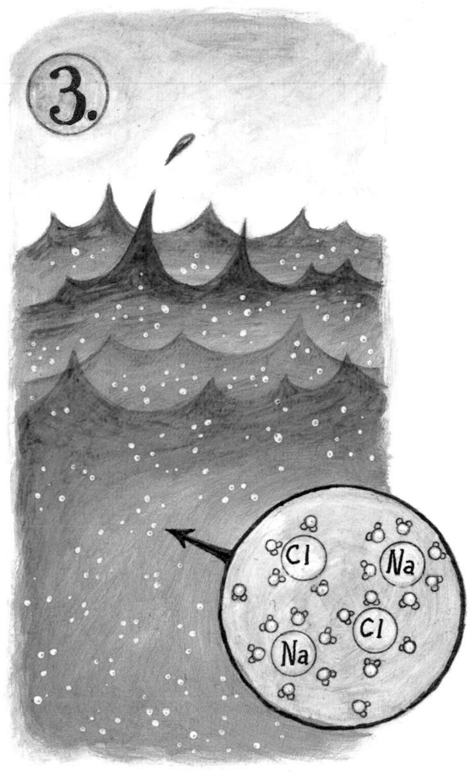

If you had all the salt in the ocean on top of a dried-out Earth, you could cover the whole planet with a layer of salt 50 meters (half a soccer field) thick.

Estuaries [Ess-(tch)yoo-AIR-eez]—Where Freshwater Rivers Meet Saltwater Oceans

As you might figure, the water there is not as salty as the rest of the ocean, and not as fresh as a running river. Water flowing through estuaries is always mixing nutrients into the soil and the sea. That makes big food webs and busy ecosystems with lots of plants, frogs, birds, and fish.

Freshwater works its way through cells in living things (like you and me) toward saltier water. Freshwater fish have body fluids that are a little saltier than the water they swim in. Freshwater works its way through their skin, and they constantly have to pump water out of their cells and out of their bodies to avoid bloating up and dying. Saltwater fish have the opposite problem. The water around them is saltier than the water in their bodies. Water tends to naturally flow out of their bodies and into the ocean. Saltwater fish gulp seawater all the time to replace the water they lose.

TRY THIS!

THE QUESTION:

How does salt get into the ocean?

HERE'S WHAT YOU NEED:

salt • water • paper towels • a measuring cup

1 Mix a spoonful of salt into 50 ml of water.
2 Pour the saltwater onto three paper towels layered on a plate.
3 Set the plate someplace sunny and warm. Wait a few days.

Amazing Ocean Currents

The world's oceans are always moving, carrying food and nutrients from one part to another. Ocean water masses move in "currents." Currents are the key to life in the sea. A current is like a giant river in the sea, and acts like an air pump bubbling oxygen into an aquarium.

Most public aquariums are built near large bodies of water—bays, sounds, or right on the ocean. To make a place like that work takes a huge flow of water. The Seattle Aquarium pumps 11,000 tons (!) of seawater through its tanks every day. It has a human-made current.

Where's that rubber duck?

The Peru Current. Flowing northward along the coast of South America, this river in the ocean is cold because its waters come up from the deepest, coldest layers of the ocean. It carries minerals from the ocean floor to the surface, which provide nutrients for huge "plumes" of plankton, which in turn provide food for billions of fish. As South American fishermen know, the Peru current has created one of the richest fishing grounds in the world.

In 1992, a ship bound from Hong Kong got stuck in a violent Pacific Ocean storm. One of the containers on the ship split open, spilling 7,220 yellow rubber ducks overboard, as well as blue turtles, green frogs, and red beaver bath toys. Many of the toys turned up in Alaska a year later. Some of them got stuck in the ice near the North Pole. Eventually, they slid into the Atlantic Ocean on the other side of the world! At first, they were just another ton of sea trash, but soon scientists realized they could use them to study a few huge ocean currents.

How Currents Work The ocean's currents are caused mainly by air. The wind rubs against the surface of the sea, and drags the water along with it. The Earth's winds move in regular patterns, and so do ocean currents. Even if the world had no wind at all, there would still be ocean currents.

Warm water, like the ocean near the Caribbean Sea, gets warmed in the tropical Sun and expands. Cooler water to the north and south squeezes the warm water up. Then water flows downhill from warmer, higher parts of the ocean to cooler, lower parts. It's like a sloshing bathtub as big as a planet.

The Gulf Stream: One of the most famous currents, it carries warm water north from the Gulf of Mexico all the way to Britain and Scandinavia—10,000 nautical miles. Then it gets pushed around by the European coast and heads back south.

Coriolis [KORR-ree-oh-liss] **Effect:** In the Northern Hemisphere, the spinning Earth pushes currents to the right. South of the equator, currents bend to the left. Scientists call this the "Coriolis effect," after the French mathematician who figured it out, Gustave Gaspard de Coriolis.

Thermohaline Currents: Sun and salt make currents—"thermohaline" [Therm-oh-HAY-leen] currents. "Thermo" means heat; "haline" means salt. Heat from the Sun makes water near the sea's surface evaporate. The salt stays put, so the surface of the sea gets saltier, and that makes the surface water heavier. It sinks and gets replaced by less salty, usually cooler, water.

The ocean is in motion.
It's the circulation of the sea that keeps everything alive.

TRY THIS!

THE QUESTION:

Does saltwater really sink?

HERE'S WHAT YOU NEED:

measuring spoon • salt • a glass of water
glass baking dish of fresh water • food coloring

1 Put 1 tablespoon of salt into a cup of water and stir it up well. Extra salt in the glass is okay.
2 Add a little food coloring. I like blue.
3 Partly fill a glass baking dish with fresh water.
4 Now slowly pour the salty water into the dish.

The salty water sinks to the bottom, and stays sunk. It's heavier than fresh (nonsalty) water. Sinking saltwater makes thermohaline flow in the ocean (currents).
BLUE
Mrs. Nye's Salt
Slowly please!

Tides Come from Outer Space

Gravity makes tides in the ocean. The Earth's gravity holds the ocean on the planet. The pull of the Moon and the pull of the Sun make the ocean bulge out a little bit toward outer space. As the Earth turns, the shores of continents and islands pass through the bulges. The level of the ocean goes up and down during the day. When you're in a bulge, it's high tide. When you're on the side next to a bulge, it's low tide.

When the Moon or the Sun pulls a bulge in the ocean on one side of the Earth, a bulge forms in the ocean on the other side of the Earth as well. The combination of the mass of the Earth with its ocean stays in balance. (So there are two high and low tides about every day.) The amount that the Earth moves in space because of the bulges is very, very small. But, it's enough to create whole ecosystems that are like nowhere else on the land or in the sea.

Highs and Lows. When the Moon and the Sun are lined up, the tides are the highest. They're called spring tides. When they're at right angles, the tides are the lowest—neap tides. One more thing—the Moon doesn't orbit the Earth right above the equator. Its orbit is tilted, so the Earth's highest and lowest tides each day are usually on opposite sides of the equator.

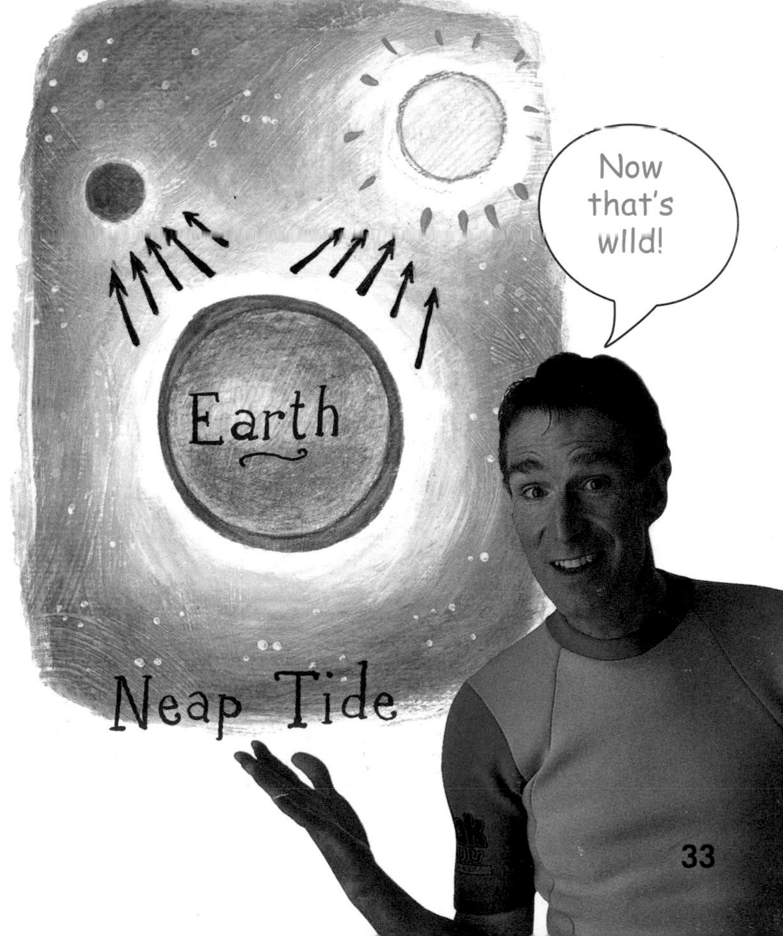

We Are Now Entering . . . the Tidal Zone

The tidal zone is where it's wet part of the time and dry part of the time. It's an unusual place to live. Plants and animals have to be able to live underwater half the time and out of water half the time. When the tide goes out, some animals, like hermit crabs, retreat to tide pools, puddles where the seawater collects. Certain creatures, like the tiny mole crab, burrow down into the damp sand and wait for the tide to come back in. Other animals, like barnacles and limpets, seal themselves inside their shells until the water returns. At low tide, the shoreline becomes a supermarket for birds. They swoop in to find food that's not underwater.

The biggest tides we know of occur in the Bay of Fundy, in the Canadian province of Nova Scotia. The level of the ocean changes as much as 17 meters (57 feet) between low and high tide. That's a tide as high as two houses!

TRY THIS!

THE QUESTION:

Where does the water go at low tide?

HERE'S WHAT YOU NEED:

a long baking dish • an empty cardboard tube • tape
a plastic drinking straw • water • blue food coloring
big felt-tip marker • scissors

1. Get a long baking dish (like the kind you make brownies in).
2. Tape an empty toilet paper tube (or half an empty paper towel tube) to the side of the dish at one end.
3. Cut the straw so that it is about as long as the pan is deep. Tape it in the corner where you can see it through the tube.
4. Fill the pan with water, and add a couple drops of blue food coloring.
5. Mark the water level on the straw with the felt-tip pen.
6. Tip the pan to one side and prop it up with a pencil or the marker. Then, mark the water level on the straw. Tip it the other way, and mark the level again. Now look through the tube. The water level changes, but it never leaves the dish—or the Earth!

Mysteries of the DEEP

We call the top layer of the ocean "the photic zone"—the layer of the ocean where sunlight penetrates. How deep sunlight gets depends on how brightly the Sun is shining and how clear the water is. Usually it's 50 to 150 meters down. Ocean plants—whether seaweed or phytoplankton—need sunlight to survive. Almost all sea plants live in the photic zone.

Deep below the surface of the ocean is where the Sun just doesn't shine. Seawater soaks up the light, so there's no photosynthesis. The sea cucumbers, plume worms, and other creatures that live on the ocean floor can eat plants and animals and dead stuff that sinks from the surface. On the other hand, most deep-sea fish are predators. They hunt each other in complete darkness. That might sound difficult at first, like a bunch of people wearing blindfolds playing hide-and-seek. But the animals of the deep sea have evolved in some pretty cool ways to live without light from above.

Lights Please. Things that live in the deep ocean make their own light. A green glow can attract other animals to meet or to eat. Showing a bright light suddenly can dazzle and confuse an attacker. Some swimming animals use an array of glowing patches for camouflage. When a predator looks up from below into the background of sunlight or moonlight, the shifting patterns of light are hard to home in on.

JAWS! Megamouth sharks and gulper eels, for example, have HUGE, HUGE jaws and mouths as wide as half their length. They have lips that glow, and they scoop food day and night in the pitch dark.

Hydrothermal Vents Scientists exploring the ocean floor discovered hydrothermal vents, cracks in the ocean floor that continually release boiling hot water from deep in the Earth's crust. Living things around hydrothermal vents don't depend directly on the Sun. Bacteria—tiny organisms—eat chemicals in the hot water to create oxygen. Small filter-feeding animals eat the bacteria, and larger animals eat the smaller animals. We end up with giant clams, mussels, and eerie red-frilled tube worms 3 meters (10 feet) long living in very hot water as far as you can get from the Sun (without drilling into the Earth!).

The oceans are deeper than the land is high. The deepest part of the ocean—a crack in the ocean floor near the Philippines called the Challenger Deep—lies 11 kilometers (7 miles) beneath the surface of the water. If you could put Mount Everest into the Challenger Deep, the top of the mountain would still be covered by 2 kilometers (over a mile) of water. Whoa!

TRY THIS!

THE QUESTION:

How does the Sun affect the ocean?

HERE'S WHAT YOU NEED:

tall glass pitcher • water • food coloring • flashlight

1 Put some water in a clear, tall glass or in a glass pitcher.
2 Add a few drops of blue food coloring and mix it up.
3 Look at a flashlight shining through the side of the glass.
4 Now hold the glass over your head.

Shine the flashlight through the side of the glass, and notice how bright it looks. Now shine the light through the top of the glass and look up from the bottom. The light looks dimmer, because it's passing through more water—the light's getting soaked up. The deeper you go in the ocean, the more water there is above you to absorb light. Try it with a long, shallow baking dish.

This helps explain why you can't see the Bahamas by dipping your face in the water in Florida!

How the Earth Rocks and Rolls

Billions of years ago, the Earth started out as a big, hot ball of molten rock. Like a chocolate chip cookie, our planet cooled from the outside surface first, forming a thin, hard rocky crust. When things cool off, they shrink (except water as it turns to ice). So the crust broke off into huge plates that move and jostle each other. The plates buckle and overlap. They slowly create mountain ranges and valleys in the seafloor that are higher than the Himalayas and deeper than the Grand Canyon.

When plates move even just a little, they can cause earthquakes. There are dozens of earthquakes every day. Most of them are underwater.

Do the Wave. A tsunami [(t)soo-NAH-mee] is a huge wave that forms when the shifting, shaking seafloor lifts and shifts the water above it. Tsunamis can make giant waves. Some are measured as high as a 10-story building. They slam millions of tons of water onto the shore, which can cause terrible damage to cities on the coast of a continent.

Do you know where the tallest mountain is? In the ocean! Mauna Kea, in Hawaii, reaches 10,203 meters (33,476 feet) from the seafloor to its tippy top, some 4,205 meters (13,796 feet) above sea level. By comparison, Mount Everest is only 8,848 meters (29,028 feet) tall. (Of course, that one is all above water.)

TRY THIS!

THE QUESTION:

How are tsunamis created?

HERE'S WHAT YOU NEED:

a plastic lid (like from a whipped cream or a large yogurt container)
string • duct tape • a bathtub • water • a few soda bottle caps

1. Attach a piece of string with tape to the center of the plastic lid, or poke a hole through the lid and tie the string on in a knot.
2. Fill the bathtub with just a little bit of water, so that the head of the tub is dry. You'll have a tub-wide beach.
3. Place one or a few upside-down soda bottle caps right on the water's edge. They are like the buildings on a beach.
4. Place the lid under water down at the tub's drain, where it's deepest.
5. Grab the string, and pull it up fast. You will create a wave.

If you do this a few times, you'll see that the up and down motion of the plastic lid creates sideways motion on the beach. Also, the wave starts out pretty small, but gets big at the shallow end. Real tsunamis caused by earthquakes do the same thing, only they often knock down things a lot bigger than bottle caps!

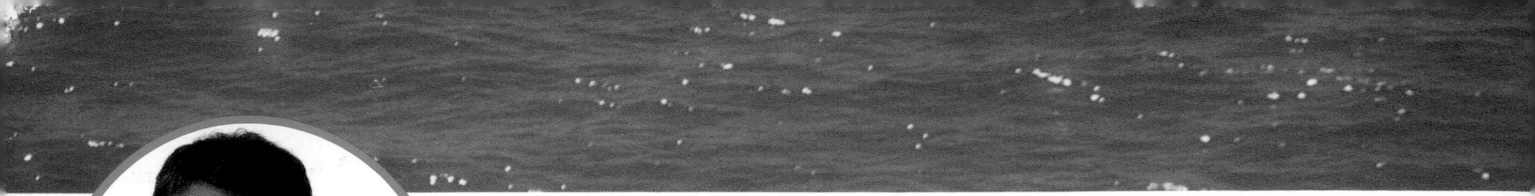

The *Ocean* and YOU

Humans explore the ocean by swimming with special equipment or building machines that can go underwater. We are inventing better and better ways to see the sea. We've built big sailing ships, submarines, diving suits, scuba gear, satellite cameras, and remote-controlled submersibles. We've learned a lot, but we've really only scratched the surface, uh . . . the bottom.

Brrr. A rusty ship is not hard to find, because saltwater is corrosive. Ocean exploration equipment has to be able to handle the salt and the cold. By human standards, most places in the ocean are not warm. In deep water, the ocean is barely above freezing, but in the Gulf of Mexico, it gets up to about 24 degrees Celsius (75 degrees Fahrenheit).

Water is heavy; it's massive. Just try hauling a bucket of it. When you dive into a pool or the ocean, the weight of the water above you creates pressure, squeezing the air out of your lungs and crushing air-filled containers—like submarines. Things that go deep have to handle a lot of pressure.

By the way, ice floats. That's why no matter how cold it gets, icebergs stay on the surface.

The Bends If we breathe pressurized air for too long, extra gas, especially nitrogen, dissolves in our blood. If we go back up to low pressure too fast, dangerous bubbles can form in our bloodstream. Divers say they feel these bubbles first in their elbows and knees (where their arms and legs bend). It's very serious, and it got named "the bends."

Scuba. Jacques Cousteau and Émile Gagnan invented the self-contained underwater breathing apparatus (scuba). They realized that we humans are mostly water. You can squeeze our bodies pretty hard with pressure, and we'll be okay. So scuba equipment supplies a diver with air under pressure. It's strong enough to fill our lungs with air even though the water around us is squeezing in.

TRY THIS!

THE QUESTION:

How can divers avoid getting "the bends"?

HERE'S WHAT YOU NEED:

2 unopened bottles of soda

1. Get two unopened bottles of soda at room temperature.
2. Shake them up.
3. Now hold one of them over the sink and twist it open fast.
4. Now get the second bottle. Twist the top slowly. Stop twisting and then twist slowly again.

The bubbles in the soda are like the dangerous bubbles a diver might get in his or her joints when he or she has not come up from the deep carefully and has the bends. Divers can avoid the bends by moving up slowly, and stopping once in a while to let the bubbles wash out of their system.

People Affect the Ocean

No matter where you go in the ocean, you will find pollution. The ocean looks huge (and it is), but it's a small world in a way. Poison from factory waste way, way inland finds its way to the sea. Oil from spills finds its way inside ocean animals as well as the humans and other animals that eat them. Would you want to eat a fish loaded with poison? Well, neither do fish. You don't have to be near the ocean to pollute it. When it rains, chemicals in fertilizers from farm fields and city garbage from landfills get carried through rivers and underground to the sea . . . see?

Not a Pretty Sight. When deep-sea exploration first became possible in the 1950s, U.S. Admiral R. J. Galanson sonar-phoned back from 11 kilometers down (7 miles deep) that he could see an empty beer can in front of him on the Pacific Ocean floor. Pollution is everywhere in the sea.

Population Explosion

Since 1900, the Earth's population has risen from about 1.5 billion to almost 6 billion humans. The level of the ocean has also risen. The Earth is kept warm by gases in our atmosphere. That's the "greenhouse effect." As more people drive cars, build factories, and use electricity (from coal and gas-burning power plants), smoggy pollution fills our skies. These gases in the air cause the greenhouse effect to get stronger than it would if we weren't burning this stuff. The world is getting warmer; the ice in the Arctic and Antarctic is melting a little, raising the level of the sea. If the Earth warms up too much, cities along the coast will just flood . . . completely.

Plastic bags aren't nutritious like good ol' mesoglea!

One Problem with Plastic. Sea turtles often confuse plastic bags with the sea jellies they like to eat, and they choke and die after eating them.

YOU Can Make a Difference!

Where do giant squid meet and mate?

Why do bacteria glow?

How much will the sea rise if the earth gets warmer?

How did animals find their way to hydrothermal vents?

How much fishing is too much fishing?

Can we farm the oceans and grow food there?

How do currents change?

Can we figure out a way to talk to whales?

By exploring and studying the ocean, we can understand our place on Earth—please see page 5. . . .

Maybe you'll be the scientist who discovers the answers to these and the tens of thousands of other questions about the ocean!

The more we know about the ocean, the better we can protect it and ourselves. Ocean scientists have lots of questions, and we need answers. The ocean affects your life, and how you live affects the ocean.

Bill Nye the Science Guy's®
GREAT BIG DINOSAUR DIG

All Bill Nye photos by Rex Rystedt; p. 18, dinosaur tracks by Kathleen W. Zoehfeld, courtesy of Robert T. Bakker; p. 34, Chicxulub images by William K. Hartman

Library of Congress Cataloging-in-Publication Data on file.

ISBN 0-7868-0542-0 (trade ed.)
ISBN 0-7868-2472-7 (lib. ed.)

I'd like to thank my parents for my genes; somehow they help me have a passion for science. But this book is for you. Your genes are just a little bit different from mine. And, your genes are just a little bit different from the deoxyribonucleic acid strands in the cells of ancient dinosaurs. Here's hoping this book helps you know a little bit more about us all. —B.N.

To anyone who ever has ever asked a question and sought its answer, this book is for you, scientists all. And to scientists past and present: the light of your curiosity continues to inspire new quests for knowledge, and to illuminate a future of possibilities. — I.S.

To J.C. —M.K.

CONTENTS

Introducing DINOSAURS, NOW & THEN

Compsognathus [Komp-sahg-NA-thuss] **must have had a nice smile—his name means "pretty jaw."**

Imagine dinosaurs as big as buses walking or wading through your neighborhood. Well, they probably did, but it was long before there were any of us humans here to see them.

Millions of years ago, there were hundreds of dinosaur species on Earth. But something changed in the environment, and all of the big walking, running, scaly-skinned dinosaurs are gone—extinct. That means they died out.

Some of the dinosaurs, a very few, found ways to survive and still thrive today. We now know them as birds. That's right; the birds flying around today are direct descendants of the ancient dinosaurs. In fact, scientists often refer to the ancient dinosaurs as "nonavian [Non AY-vee-uhn] dinosaurs." That just means "dinosaurs that are not birds."

CHECK IT OUT!

Brachiosaurus [BRAK-ee-uh-Sorr-uss] was as huge as any land animal could be, five stories high and as heavy as two trailer trucks. Phew.

Paleozoic Era 540 million years ago | Mesozoic Era 245 million years ago | TRIASSIC PERIOD begins (Age of Dinosaurs begins)

It's hard to imagine just how old ancient dinosaur fossils are.

Follow this time line along the bottom of every page to see how many millions of years it took for you to come into the picture.

Eoraptor **230** million years ago

The best way to learn about dinosaurs is to dig. We look for fossils. Fossils can be bones, patterns of bones or plants, footprints, or traces of skin. Ancient dinosaur fossils tell us about amazing creatures that once lived on Earth. When we compare dinosaur and plant fossils from ancient times to animals and plants living today, we learn more about how plants and animals fit together in ecosystems. After all, ancient dinosaurs were animals just like you and me. Well, not *exactly* like you and me.

How many people do you know who would gladly eat a whole horse . . . or a few worms?

So You Want to Be a Dinosaur Scientist We call scientists who study dinosaurs "paleontologists" [Pay-lee-en-TAHL-uh-jists]. Paleontology is the study of living things so old that there were no humans around to see or record them. And new discoveries are being made all the time, so paleontology is constantly changing. Until late in the twentieth century, hardly anyone thought birds were dinosaurs. But it sure looks that way now.

TRY THIS!

THE QUESTION:

How did such huge creatures hold themselves up?

HERE'S WHAT YOU NEED:

four bars of modeling clay, about 100 grams (3½ oz.) each
a ½-liter plastic bottle • a 1-liter plastic bottle • a 2-liter plastic bottle
(each bottle should be filled with water and closed with a cap)

1 Take half of one clay bar and cut it in half again. Shape each piece into an upside-down V. Then set the ½-liter bottle on the two Vs, to make a standing "Bottleosaurus."

2 Use a plastic knife or even an old credit card to cut one bar of clay in half the long way to make two pairs of legs about 20 centimeters (8 inches) long. Set the 1-liter bottle on them.

3 Now, use the last two bars of clay to make two big pairs of legs. Using the 2-liter bottle, make an even bigger and heavier model dinosaur that stands twice as high.

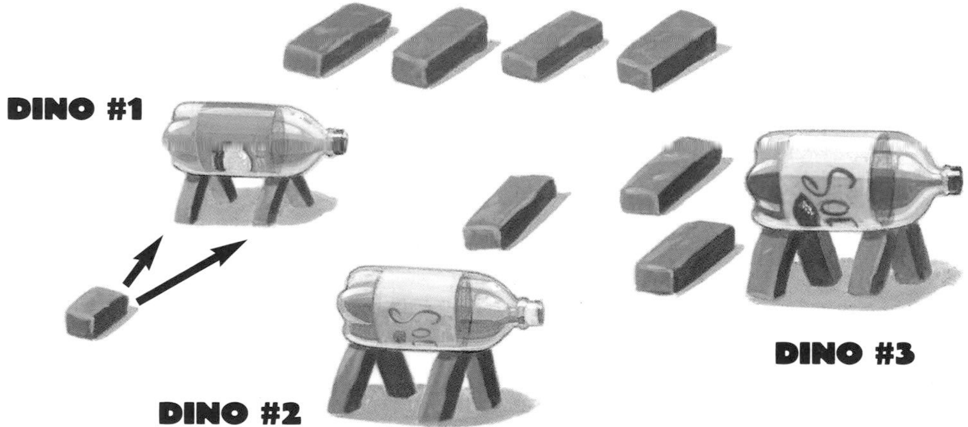

As animals get bigger, their legs have to get much thicker. That's why ants can have thin, wiry legs, but rhinoceroses need big, thick ones, like tree trunks. The same is true of animals like you, me, and *Tyrannosauruses.*

How Do We Know WHAT DINOSAURS LOOKED LIKE?

Well, we don't, exactly.

Plateosaurus [Platt-ee-uh-SORR-uss] **got around! His is one of the most commonly found dinosaur fossils in Europe, with discoveries in more than 50 different sites.**

No human has ever seen an ancient dinosaur—let alone taken a photo of one or painted one on a cave wall. But we can start figuring out what they looked like by studying their bones and the bones of birds. First of all, dinosaurs had ankles that are different from those of other reptiles. Dinosaur ankles could work like the hinge on a lunch-box lid, just one way. Humans can swing their ankles forward and backward. We can also move them side to side. Well, ancient dinosaurs couldn't do that, and neither can birds.

Scientists also look at animal hip joints. Ancient dinosaurs walked with their legs right under their bodies. So do birds. Other reptiles, like crocodiles, have their legs splayed out at their sides.

Our human hips swivel with a ball in a socket. You can get an idea of how these shapes fit together by clenching the fingers of one hand into a fist. Then hold your fist with your other hand. Your fist is the ball; your other hand is the socket. But in ancient dinosaurs and birds, the hip socket usually has a hole in it. So, it's shaped like a doughnut. Scientists carefully examine dinosaur bones to try to see how all the bones fit together.

Assembling bones from a fossil dig into a dinosaur skeleton is just like putting a jigsaw puzzle together. Well, it's not quite so easy. Dinosaurs weren't flat; they had muscles and skin, which we can't see. And there's no picture on the box to show you what the dinosaur is supposed to look like when you're done!

By building dinosaur skeletons, scientists get a pretty good idea of how tall dinosaurs were, whether they stood on two or four feet, and about how big their brains were compared to their bodies.

Camouflage Most animals have coloring that helps them blend in with their surroundings. This coloring, called camouflage [KAM-uh-Flahzh], helps animals hide from predators or sneak up on their prey. We see masked raccoons, striped zebras, patchy and splotched whales, and snakes with patterns like international flags. So it could be that ancient dinosaurs had wild patterns and colors as well. What do you think?

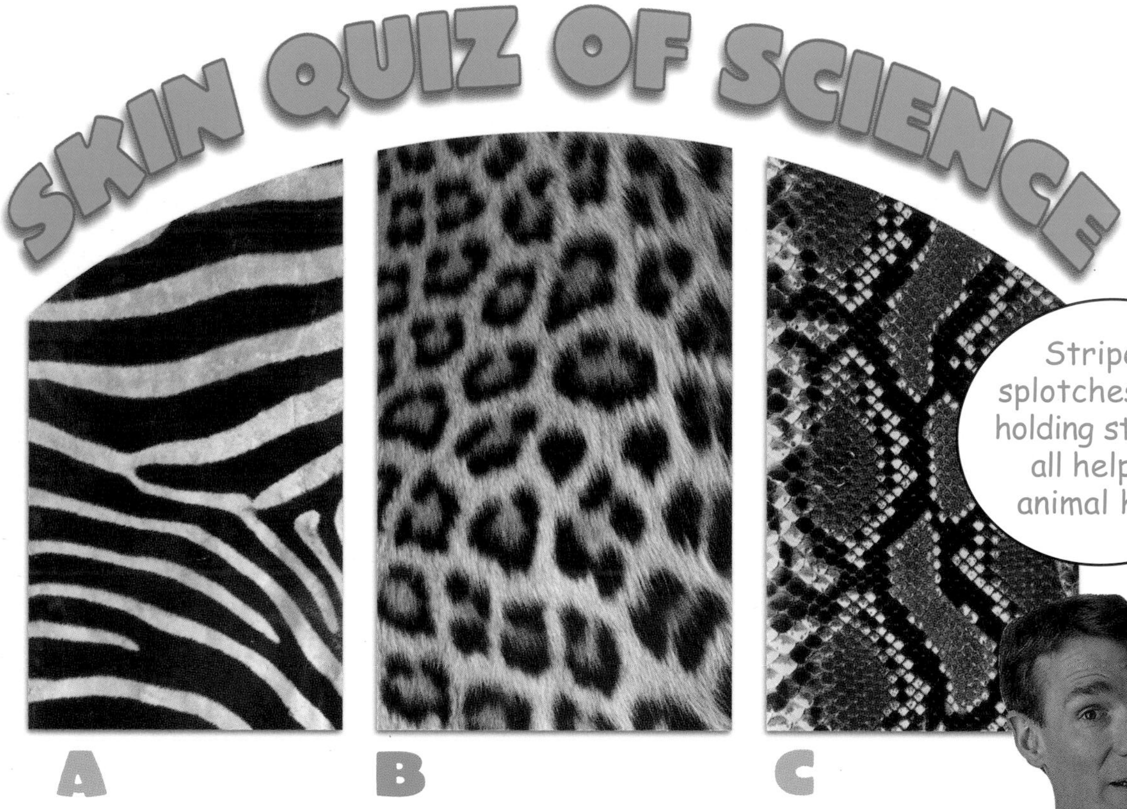

SKIN QUIZ OF SCIENCE

A

B

C

Stripes, splotches, and holding still can all help an animal hide.

CHECK IT OUT!

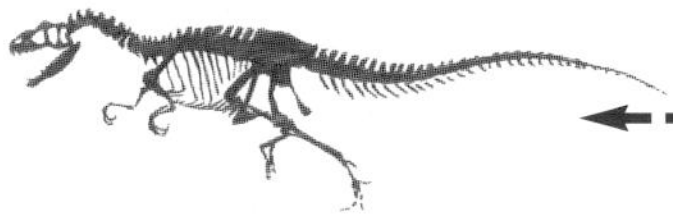

In 1842, Richard Owen made up the word *dinosaur*, meaning "fearfully big lizard."

A Zebra
B Leopard
C Snake

TRY THIS!

THE QUESTION:

How did dinosaurs use camouflage to hide?

HERE'S WHAT YOU NEED:

a balloon (try a green or tan one) • tempera paints
a place to hide (like the woods, a sandy area, or your backyard)

1. Blow up your balloon and pretend it's a dinosaur (a Balloonosaurus?).
2. Decide what kind of environment your Balloonosaurus lives in. The woods? The grass? A sandy desert? Or perhaps on a barren rocky slope?
3. Paint your Balloonosaurus to blend into your environment. Try brown, green, yellow, and black splotches for a forest. If you want to hide in dry grass, try tan and black stripes, like a tiger.

Camouflage isn't perfect, but it doesn't have to be. After you get a pattern worked out, see if a friend can find your Balloonosaurus in, say, a minute. That's plenty of time for an animal to plan an escape or an attack.

Pachycephalosaurus [Pak-ee-SEFF-uh-luh-Sorr-uss] was a real blockhead. He had a head like a dome with a very thick skull, up to 25 centimeters (10 inches) thick!

FORMING A FOSSIL

Fossils provide evidence that ancient dinosaurs once lived. Most fossils were formed when animals died and got buried by earth that was moved by winds or floods. When the buried animals and the soil around them got very wet, minerals in the soil worked their way into the bones. Sometimes, chemical reactions changed the composition of the bones, making them as hard as rocks, and preserving the tiny details of the bone shapes. We call this "permineralization" [per-MIN-(uh)-ril-ih-Zay-shun].

If the conditions are just right, the permineralized bones are not dissolved away as they lie in the ground, and the loose soil and sand that once surrounded the bones harden into rock. Since the bones are still inside, the animal or trace of animal is preserved within the solid rock.

Paleontologists have learned how to look for rocks that might hold fossils. They usually find one edge or end of a bone, then start digging into the earth around that spot. In general, things that are buried at the same depth in a layer of rock or dirt are about the same age. To get to most fossils, scientists have to chip away very carefully at solid rocks. Phew.

People have been digging up fossils for centuries. Thousands of years ago, Greek people found fossils of giraffes that had gone extinct millions of years earlier. But our modern dinosaur digging really took off when scientists in Europe started to find bones and teeth of large mysterious reptiles in the early 1800s.

TRY THIS!

THE QUESTION:

How do bones become permineralized?

HERE'S WHAT YOU NEED:

an old sponge • salt • a big glass of warm water • a spoon • a saucer

1. Add 50 milliliters (3 tablespoons) of salt to the glass of warm water. Stir it until most of the salt disappears.
2. Soak your sponge in this salty, salty water. Squeeze and resoak the sponge to work the salty water all the way through.
3. Tip the glass and gently drain away the excess water.
4. Slide your permineralized salt sponge onto the plate and let it dry for a few days. If you want, you can bury it in some sand, and let it dry there like a fossil bone in the earth.

When you pick it up (or dig it up), you can feel that it's solid and stiff as a rock. Look at it closely in bright light, and you'll see sparkly mineral crystals.

Your sponge has become "permineralized"—a lot like a fossil dinosaur bone.

TYRANNOSAURUS REX

Digging Up BONES

Tyrannosaurus rex [tih-RAN-ih-Sorr-uss] had teeth as much as 23 centimeters (9 inches) long and could eat 1/4 ton in one bite!

In general, places that are wet today don't hold many dinosaur fossils. The flow of water is always shifting things around, carrying them away, and dissolving them for good. Fossils are preserved when they are buried in soil that can withstand sun and rain for millions of years.

Animals hang out where there's water to drink and plants to eat. So, when we go looking for fossils, we often look in places where there used to be water—ancient riverbeds, gorges, gulches, or canyons that have dried out.

By looking closely at dinosaur bones, we can come up with theories about their behavior. For example, many *Tyrannosaurus* skeletons have been found with healed broken ribs. And from their skeletons, we also know that they had very short arms. A few scientists figured that if a *Tyrannosaurus* fell down, he could get badly hurt, because he couldn't break his fall by extending an arm as, say, a human can. So it could be that they didn't run any faster than the speed at which they could safely fall.

This is just one possible explanation for the cracked rib bones in the rocks. What do you think?

The material encasing a fossil is called the "matrix" [MAY-tricks]. The rock or soil you have to dig down through to get to a fossil is called the "overburden."

TRY THIS!

THE QUESTION:

How do you get a fossil out of a rock without damaging it?

HERE'S WHAT YOU NEED:

a chicken bone or two • plaster of Paris • 2 paper buckets or large paper cups • old toothbrush • safety glasses

1 Next time you eat a piece of chicken, save a bone or two. Then clean the meat off of them and let them dry for a few days.
2 Mix up the plaster of Paris in one of the cups. Pour about half of the mixture into the other cup.
3 Set the bone(s) in the plaster of the second cup; then cover it up to the top with the rest of the plaster. You could also have a friend set the bone(s) in the plaster, so you don't know exactly where it is in the bucket.
4 Let the plaster harden for several hours or, better yet, a couple of days.
5 Peel the bucket away and then see how easy (uh, difficult) it is to get a fossil out of a rock. You may have to use a hammer and chisel. Protect your eyes with safety glasses if you do. If you don't have a chisel, try a rock that has a sharp edge.

To remove the bone cleanly, you have to scrape the plaster off and then, very carefully, brush it away using the toothbrush.

Seismosaurus [SIZE-muh-Sorr-uss] was one of the longest land animals that has ever existed, at 40–50 meters (130–170 feet).

Making Tracks

Not all dinosaur fossils are bones. Scientists have found dinosaur tracks and traces of dinosaurs' digestive systems and respiratory tracts (breathing tubes and lungs).

Dinosaur tracks help us answer a whole new set of questions: How much did she weigh? Did he walk on two feet or four? Did she drag her tail when she ran? We look at the depth of the prints and the spacing between prints. We can also look closely at how deeply the toes or heels dug in to understand if the dinosaur was hurrying or strolling through some ancient muddy spot.

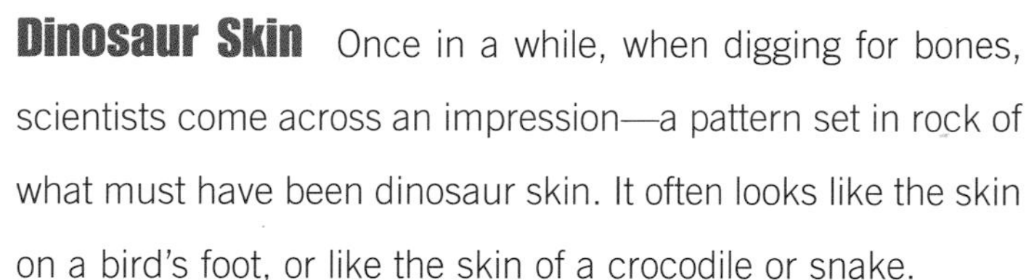

Dinosaur Skin Once in a while, when digging for bones, scientists come across an impression—a pattern set in rock of what must have been dinosaur skin. It often looks like the skin on a bird's foot, or like the skin of a crocodile or snake.

We find dinosaur tracks all around the world. They were formed when animals walked through mud, maybe near a swamp or bog. Then the whole area had to dry out before the prints were wiped away by weather, like rain. And the dried-out rocky area has to be where humans can stumble upon them millions of years later.

Think about walking through a muddy spot near where you live. How long do you think it would be before someone or something else came through and destroyed the impressions you had left? Probably not long. Unlikely as it may seem, there are many places in the world where we've found dinosaur "trackways," places where ancient dinosaurs left footprints. Trackways are usually in deserts, places that are now very, very dry, but were once part of completely different ecosystems.

We can go see the tracks of a giant herbivore in Texas. Right alongside them there are the tracks of a smaller carnivore. Maybe the meat-seeker was hunting the big plant-chewer. We can't tell exactly what happened; but like each fossil we find, every trackway tells a story.

153 million years ago *Camptosaurus*

TRY THIS!

THE QUESTION:

What do we learn from dinosaur trackways?

HERE'S WHAT YOU NEED:

a long roll of paper (about 5 meters, or 15 feet)
tempera paint any color • an old baking pan or dish

1. Roll the paper out on a lawn or sidewalk.
2. Pour some paint in the dish.
3. Take off your shoes and socks, step in the dish, then walk on the paper. Try running, walking on your hands, or crab walking, with your stomach up and hands behind you.
4. To study it later, hang it on your wall.

By looking at the patterns of your trackways, you can tell how you or your friends (Humanosauruses?) were getting around, and how quickly. That's what scientists do with trackways.

Short, Tall, *Fast*, & SLOW—

They Were Everywhere, You Know!

Ankylosaurus [ang-KYLE-uh-Sorr-uss] had great built-in protection from his predators, with thick, armorlike skin, large horns on the back of his head, and a clublike tail.

Every year, scientists unearth fossils of new ancient dinosaurs. We find about seven new species each year. They came in all shapes and sizes, like the animals of today—though there aren't any land animals today nearly as big as even the medium-size ancient dinosaurs. A *Seismosaurus* [SIZE-muh-Sorr-uss] weighed as much as ten elephants. But the largest animals that have ever lived on Earth are still around today—blue whales. They can get as big as they are because their bodies are supported by water.

Birds did not actually come from what early paleontologists called the bird-hipped dinosaurs. That's the way science goes sometimes.

Dinosaurs are divided into two groups, depending on their hip structure.

SAURISCHIANS

One group had hips like lizards. The big hip-bone called the "pubis" [PYOO-biss] went forward. We call these dinosaurs saurischians [Sorr-ISH-ee-inz], meaning "lizard-hipped."

Scientists further divide the saurischians into two groups, depending on the type of feet they had.

Sauropods [SORR-uh-Pahdz] had "lizard feet."

Theropods [THAIR-uh-Pahdz] had "beast feet." Their feet were fitted with big, sharp claws. These theropods are the ancestors of the birds we see flying and running around today.

SAURISCHIAN

Ischium

Pubis

ORNITHISCHIANS

The other group of dinosaurs had hips that made early scientists think of birds. We call them "ornithischians" [Or-nih-THISH-ee-inz], "bird-hipped," even though they didn't turn out to be the ancestors of birds. Their pubis bones pointed backward.

ORNITHISCHIAN

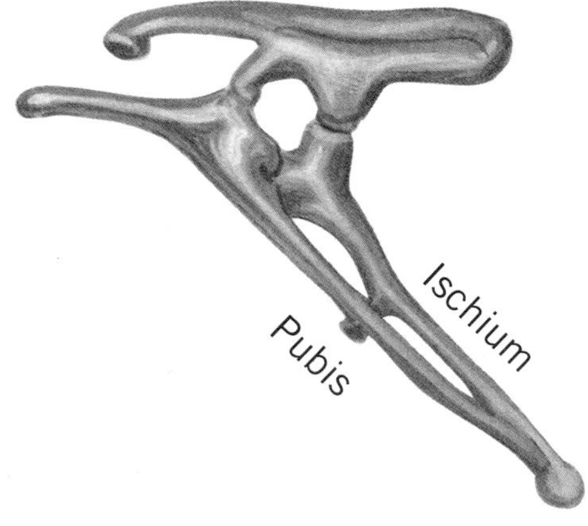

Warm-blooded, Cold-blooded, or Both? You and I are what we call "warm-blooded." We keep the same body temperature all day. Being warm-blooded allows us to move pretty fast, even when it's cold out. Modern reptiles are what we call "cold-blooded." Their body temperatures go up and down with the temperature of their surroundings. So, it takes time for a cold-blooded animal to rev up after a cool night.

Scientists are still debating whether the ancient dinosaurs were cold-blooded or warm-blooded. Birds are warm-blooded, so it would make sense that dinosaurs were as well. But, on the other hand, reptiles are cold-blooded, and dinosaurs had a lot in common with them, too. Maybe you'll be the scientist who figures it out.

On Earth right now, there are also animals that show characteristics of being both warm-blooded and cold-blooded. Leatherback sea turtles (which are reptiles) keep the same temperature all the time. And African naked mole-rats (which are mammals) let their body temperature go way down at night. So maybe some dinosaurs were warm-blooded and others were cold-blooded.

IT'S TIME TO PLAY . . .
"WHAT'S MY BODY TEMPERATURE?"

TRY THIS!

THE QUESTION:

What does it mean to be warm-blooded?

HERE'S WHAT YOU NEED:

a thermometer • a shower or bathtub

1. Measure the temperature inside your body with a thermometer under your tongue. For most of us, it's about 37.0 degrees Celsius (98.6 degrees Fahrenheit).
2. Now, take a cold shower for a couple of minutes. You'll feel cold when the water hits your chest, your "core." Then, measure your body temperature again.
3. Now, take a hot shower, or get in a hot bath. Measure your temperature.
4. Try running around until you're hot and sweaty. What's your temperature now?

Although your skin temperature changes a bit, your inside body temperature stays the same. You're warm-blooded.

IGUANODON

WHAT'S FOR DINNER?

Iguanodon [ih-GWAN-uh-dahn] earned his name by having teeth that are similar to those of an iguana. Ancient dinosaurs had to eat, just like you and me.

If you think about it, figuring out what an animal likes to eat tells a lot about his or her behavior. Scientists like to divide animals into three categories, according to what they eat: meat eaters, plant eaters, or some-of-each–eaters. We call them carnivores [KAR-nih-vorz], herbivores [HERB-ih-vorz], and omnivores [AHM-nih-vorz]. You may have eaten Mexican pork strips called *carnitas.* Then you're a meat eater. Or you may have enjoyed food seasoned with bits of leaves or "herbs." Then you're a plant eater. Most humans eat both meat and plants. We're omnivores. In Latin, *omni* means "all" or "everything."

MENU

MENU

125 million years ago *Utahraptor*

We can figure out what ancient dinosaurs must have eaten by taking a close look at their teeth. Carnivores have long, sharp, tearing teeth. Herbivores can have sharp, scissorlike teeth in the front and flat teeth with low tough ridges for grinding plants in the back.

Inspect a cat's choppers, and you'll find carnivorous [Kar-NIH-ver-uss] teeth. Check behind a cow's lips and you'll see herbivorous [Hir-BIH-ver-uss] grinder teeth. Open your mouth in front of the mirror, and you'll find that you have sharp teeth in front and low, strong grinding teeth in back.

JURASSIC SPECIALS
FOR HERBIVORES
SAUTÉED FERNS IN A DELICATE RIVER-WATER SAUCE
FOR OMNIVORES
SAUTÉED FERNS OR ANY NEIGHBORING ANIMAL
FOR CARNIVORES
ANY DINOSAUR AT YOUR TABLE (PLEASE DON'T EAT YOUR WAITER!)
MENU

The majority of animals, now and in ancient times, eat plants. These herbivores need lots and lots of plants to feed on. Carnivores usually eat herbivores. If there are too many carnivores in an ecosystem, pretty soon there isn't enough food to go around. Scientists often think of ecosystems as being a food pyramid with tons and tons of plants at the bottom, plenty of herbivores in the middle, then just a few meat-eating predators at the top.

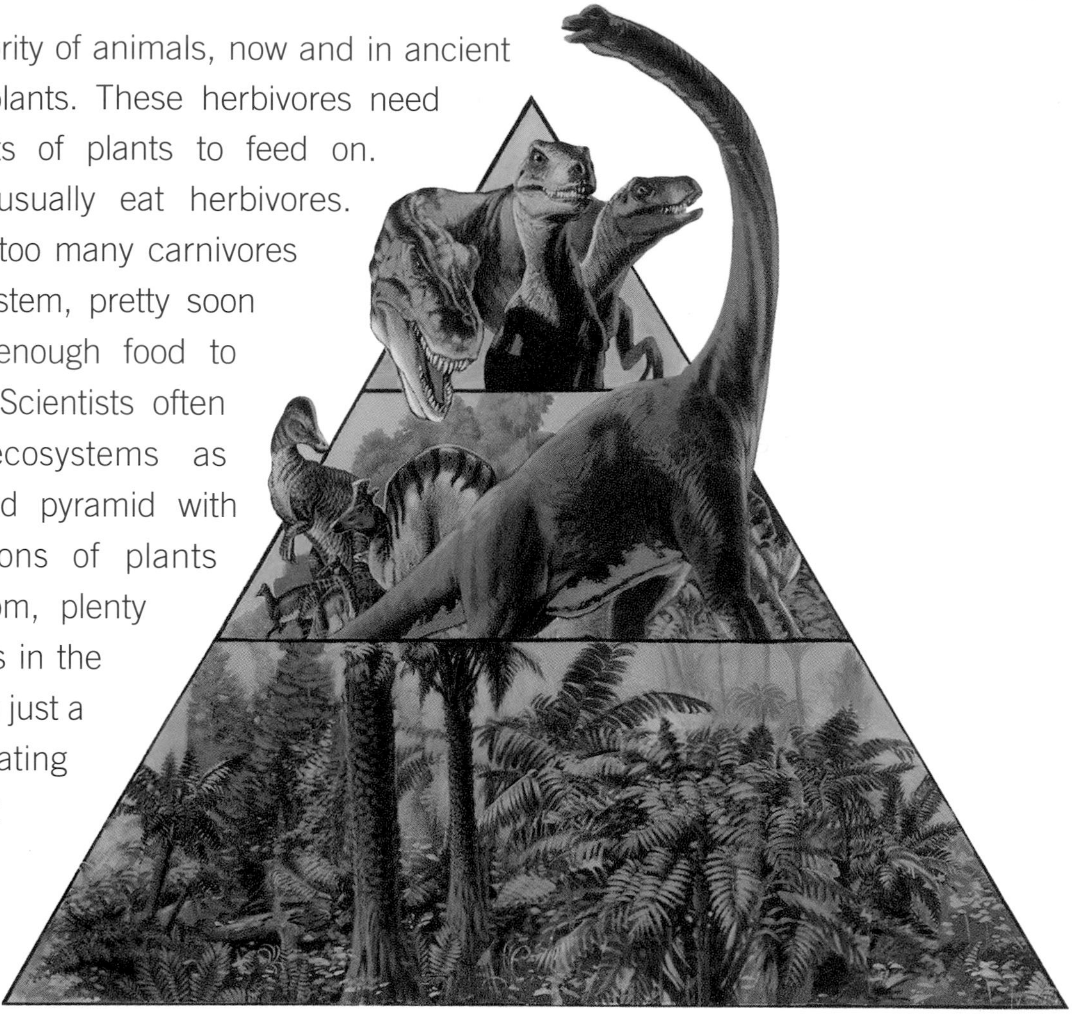

Raptors Animals with big claws or talons [TAL-unz] are often called "raptors" [RAP-torz]. That means "robbers" in Latin. Nowadays the only living raptors are birds. What do animals do with talons? Well, they catch animals and eat them. If you eat plants, you don't have the problem of your food running away. So, when scientists found the bones of what must have been a very fast-running carnivore, they called it *"Velociraptor"* [veh-LAHSS-ih-Rapp-ter], a raptor with velocity, or speed.

TRY THIS!

THE QUESTION:

Are you a carnivore, herbivore, or omnivore?

HERE'S WHAT YOU NEED:

meat foods • vegetable foods

1. Try eating only meat for a whole day. Have, say, sausage or bacon for breakfast, bologna for lunch, and chicken for dinner. That means no bread, no potato chips, no pickles or lettuce, mustard, or ketchup for a whole day. You'll probably find yourself hankering for some crunchy celery or smooth peanut butter before long.

2. Try eating only vegetables for a day. Have peas, carrots, spinach, beans, and potato chips. To be a real herbivore, you shouldn't have any milk, cheese, or fish. Those all come from animals.

Time, Time, & more TIME

Eoraptor [Ee-oh-RAPP-ter] is the oldest carnivorous dinosaur fossil found so far.

Your parents might be about thirty years older than you are. Your grandparents might be about sixty years older than you are. But the fossils of the ancient dinosaurs are 65 million years older than anyone alive today.

Dinosaurs started living on the earth about 230 million years ago, and most of them died out 65 million years ago. We figured this out by careful, careful study of the rocks in which dinosaur fossil bones were found. There are a few different ways that scientists can figure out how old dinosaur fossils are.

Over time, rocks on the Earth's surface pile up in layers. Scientists call each layer of rock a "stratum" [STRAT-uhm]; multiple layers are called "strata" [STRAT-uh]. By looking at the type of rock, where it is on the Earth's surface, and the thickness of each stratum, scientists figure out how old the layers are. If you find a fossil in a particular stratum, then you know about how old it is. This is the oldest (and still very good) way to date fossils. We call the study of strata "stratigraphy" [stra-TIG-ruh-fee]. Usually, the deeper a fossil is buried, the longer it's been there.

Another method of dating fossils is studying the rocks in which they are found. Rocks have many different minerals in them, one of which is potassium [poh-TASS-ee-um]. It's made of tiny particles called atoms [AT-umz]. Each potassium atom has nineteen almost unimaginably even tinier particles inside it called protons [PRO-tahnz]. As these atoms age, they lose a proton, ending up with only eighteen. Then, they become a completely different substance called argon [AR-gahn].

106 million years ago — Dinosaurs thrive in what is now Antarctica

Many dinosaur fossils are buried under the ash of volcanoes that erupted millions of years ago. After the ash is tossed up onto the surface from Earth's core, the potassium atoms in the ash slowly decay and change into argon. Scientists have learned to predict how long it takes for this to happen. By carefully measuring how much potassium and argon are in the soil around fossils, we can calculate how long ago a fossil was buried. By the way, volcanoes are still erupting today, and once in a while, plants and animals are buried. They might someday become fossils, too.

Radioactive minerals inside the Earth help us date fossils.

Eras and Periods Scientists who study the Earth, who are called geologists [Jee-ahL-uh-jists], have figured out that our planet has gone through different ages of time. The first block of time is called the Paleozoic [Pay-lee-uh-ZOH-ik] Era, or "ancient time." But the ancient dinosaurs lived in what's called the Mesozoic [MEZ-uh-Zoh-ik] Era, the "middle time." We live in the era after the Mesozoic, called the Cenozoic [Sen-uh-ZOH-ic] Era. It means "recent time."

After carefully studying the layers of rock and soil in the Earth's crust, geologists have gone on to subdivide the Mesozoic Era into three smaller periods: First was the Triassic [try-ASS-ik] Period, which was the time when dinosaurs first appeared. Then, there was the Jurassic [jer-ASS-ik] Period, which occurred in the middle of the Mesozoic Era. It's named after the Jura mountains in Europe, where the layers of rock from this period were discovered. The latest or more recent period was the Cretaceous [krih-TAY-shiss]. That means chalky; it was first understood by studying chalky rocks. Different kinds of dinosaurs lived during all three periods of the Mesozoic Era.

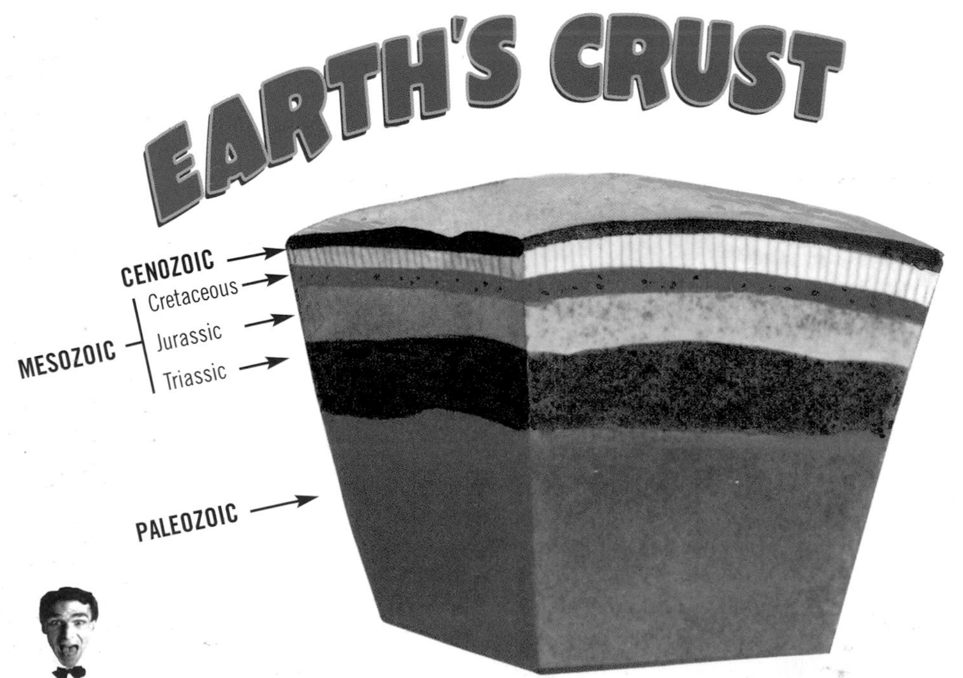

CHECK IT OUT!

Many dinosaurs never saw a flower or bit into fruit from a tree. There were no flowers until the Cretaceous Period. Before that, it was all ferns, ferns, ferns.

TRY THIS!

THE QUESTION:

How much time has passed since dinosaurs were around?

HERE'S WHAT YOU NEED:

a 500-sheet package of paper • drawing pencils, markers, or crayons

1. Write "*Giganotosaurus*" [jie-gan-NAH-tuh-Sorr-uss] at the very top of the first page of the stack of paper. That's the start of your Pages of Time. The stack of paper represents 100 million years. Each side of each page represents 100,000 years.
2. The ancient dinosaurs became extinct 65 million years ago. You can mark that 175 pages after Giganotosaurus.
3. Now, go to the bottom of the back of the very last sheet of paper. That's where we come in. The last Ice Age ended about 25,000 years ago. That would be a fourth of the way down the back of the last page. Fold the paper there and mark it. The pyramids in Egypt were built around five thousand years ago. Mark that on the same page just 14 millimeters (9⁄16 inch) from the bottom. Almost all of human recorded history—every newspaper, movie, photograph, king, queen, president, and actor lived below this line. So do you and I.
4. If you live to be 90 years old, your whole life will fit in a pencil line just 0.25 millimeter (1⁄100 inch) wide right on the bottom edge of the back of the last page.

That's a lot of pages.

That's a lot of time!

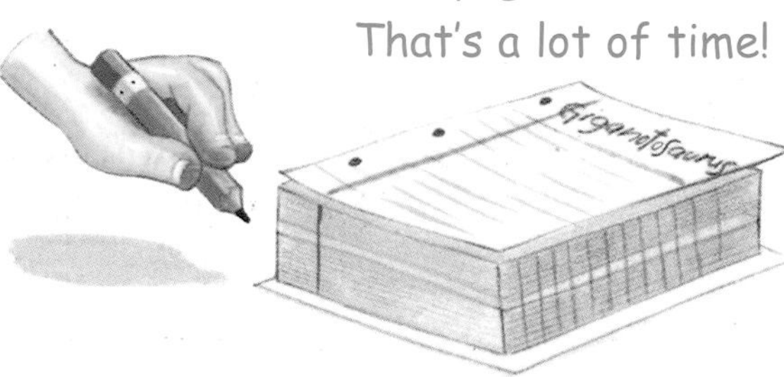

TRICERATOPS

Where Did
All the Ancient Dinosaurs Go?

Triceratops [Trie-SAIR-uh-tops] had three horns and a "frilly" bony plate behind his face. Of course his "frills" weighed more than a refrigerator.

You and I are surrounded by living things. And every living thing affects the others around it. Ancient dinosaurs lived in the same kind of world. But 65 million years ago, something happened that made almost all the dinosaurs disappear. For a long time, scientists have reasoned that most of these magnificent animals must have stopped fitting into their changing environment. They may have been slowly disappearing by the end of the Mesozoic Era.

But until the mid-1980s, no one had a good theory, or idea, of how so many of the dinosaurs could have disappeared at once. Now, many scientists agree that the ancient dinosaurs were killed by meteors, or rocks, from outer space. They figured this out by looking not only at fossils but also at the rocks and soil in which they were buried.

Wherever we find fossils from the last dinosaurs of 65 million years ago, we also find a layer of unusual metal. It's shiny like silver, and it doesn't rust. Similar to chromium (which makes chrome car parts shiny), it's called iridium [ih-RIH-dee-um]. On Earth it is quite rare, but it's pretty common in rocks that have fallen from outer space.

At about the same time that Earth and the other planets were formed by gravity pulling particles of stardust together, much smaller bits of rock and ice

75 million years ago *Corythosaurus*

also formed. (When I say smaller, I mean anywhere from the size of a speck of dust to the size of a city!) When these rocks slam into Earth's atmosphere and trail a bright streak through the sky, we call them meteors **[MEE-tee-urz]**. If they make it all the way to the ground or the sea, we call them "meteorites" **[MEE-tee-ur-Ites]**.

Sixty-five million years ago, a meteorite or group of meteorites about 15 kilometers (10 miles) across came slamming into Earth from outer space. Traveling very fast, at least 11 kilometers per second (almost 40,000 kilometers per hour), they hit the ground with a lot of energy. That energy had to go somewhere, so it probably caused a huge explosion, a fireball of molten (melted) rock. The force of the wind alone would have blown animals and trees right over. The flying debris became a worldwide dust cloud. When the dust settled, it left a layer of iridium all over the place. Now, scientists find a layer of iridium buried just above the layer containing the last of the Cretaceous dinosaurs.

With all that smoke and dust in the air, light and heat from the Sun were probably reflected back into space. So green plants that needed the sunlight to grow died out. The very large animals that depended on plants to eat died out also. A few of them mangaged to survive, and their descendants are still around today.

Chicxulub In 1982, geologists looking for oil under the Gulf of Mexico noticed a big ring of magnetic rock that was affecting their compasses. They reported it, but no one took much notice. Three years later, scientists looking at images from satellites orbiting high above Earth's surface noticed the same ring. It is near Chicxulub [CHEEKS-uh-loob], Mexico. This huge ring is about 200 kilometers across. It's now called the Chicxulub Crater, and it is almost certainly the place where the meteorite landed that might have killed many sea plants and animals. It may have also killed the ancient dinosaurs.

Now, that's wild!

Look Up! It is very possible that Earth will one day be hit by another meteorite as big as the one in Chicxulub. It would certainly change our world as we know it. But forward-thinking people could design and build a missile or other system to slam into a rock in space so that it would miss our home planet. Should we spend billions of tax dollars, euros, and yen to build a "deflector system"? The price of not doing it might be bigger than we can figure.

73 million years ago *Tyrannosaurus* — **72** million years ago *Parasaurolophus* — **71** million years ago *Thescelosaurus* — **68** million years ago *Torosaurus* — **67** million years ago *Edmontosaurus*

TRY THIS!

THE QUESTION:

How can dust affect the temperature?

HERE'S WHAT YOU NEED:

two big, thick books • a pencil • a thermometer
a bright reading light • plastic wrap • adhesive tape • flour

1. Place two books on a table about 30 centimeters (1 foot) apart.
2. Place a pencil on the table pointing from one book to another.
3. Set one end of the thermometer on top of the pencil, at a right angle to it.
4. Stretch a sheet of plastic wrap over the whole thing. Tape the plastic wrap to the table on both sides. Shine the light on the books, pencil, and thermometer.
5. Wait five minutes, then write down the temperature.
6. Now sprinkle some flour on the plastic wrap. Wait five more minutes. Watch the temperature.
7. Brush the flour away. Wait five minutes, then check the temperature again.

The flour is like the dust that was thrown into the atmosphere from Chicxulub 65 million years ago.

PANGAEA, One Big World

Argentinosaurus's [arr-jen-TEEN-uh-Sorr-uss] **fossil was discovered in guess what country?**

When you look at Earth from space, or maybe just on a globe, you will notice that Africa looks as if it could fit right into South America, just like pieces of a puzzle. It turns out, they once did fit together.

Scientists have found fossils of *Titanosaurs* [tie-TAN-uh-Sorz] in Asia, Europe, and South America. Yet these continents are separated by thousands of kilometers of ocean. Dinosaur fossils helped us discover how the land we live on moves around.

All of the land on our planet used to be fused into one gigantic piece that we now refer to as "Pangaea" [pan-JEE-uh]. That means "all the world." The entire surface, or crust, of our world is made of huge rocky slabs that we call "tectonic" [tek-TAHN-ik] plates. Tectonic means "builder." By carefully studying earthquakes, mountains, valleys, and volcanoes, scientists have figured out where one plate is bumping into another and which plates are moving in what direction.

Before the continents began to separate and the sea started sloshing over the land, dinosaurs could walk from one tectonic plate to another. That is why we now find fossils of many of the same dinosaurs all over the world. Back then, the ocean was shallower. It covered more of Earth's surface, so the Earth could hold more heat from the Sun. This warmth helped more plants grow, so there was more food around for dinosaurs to eat.

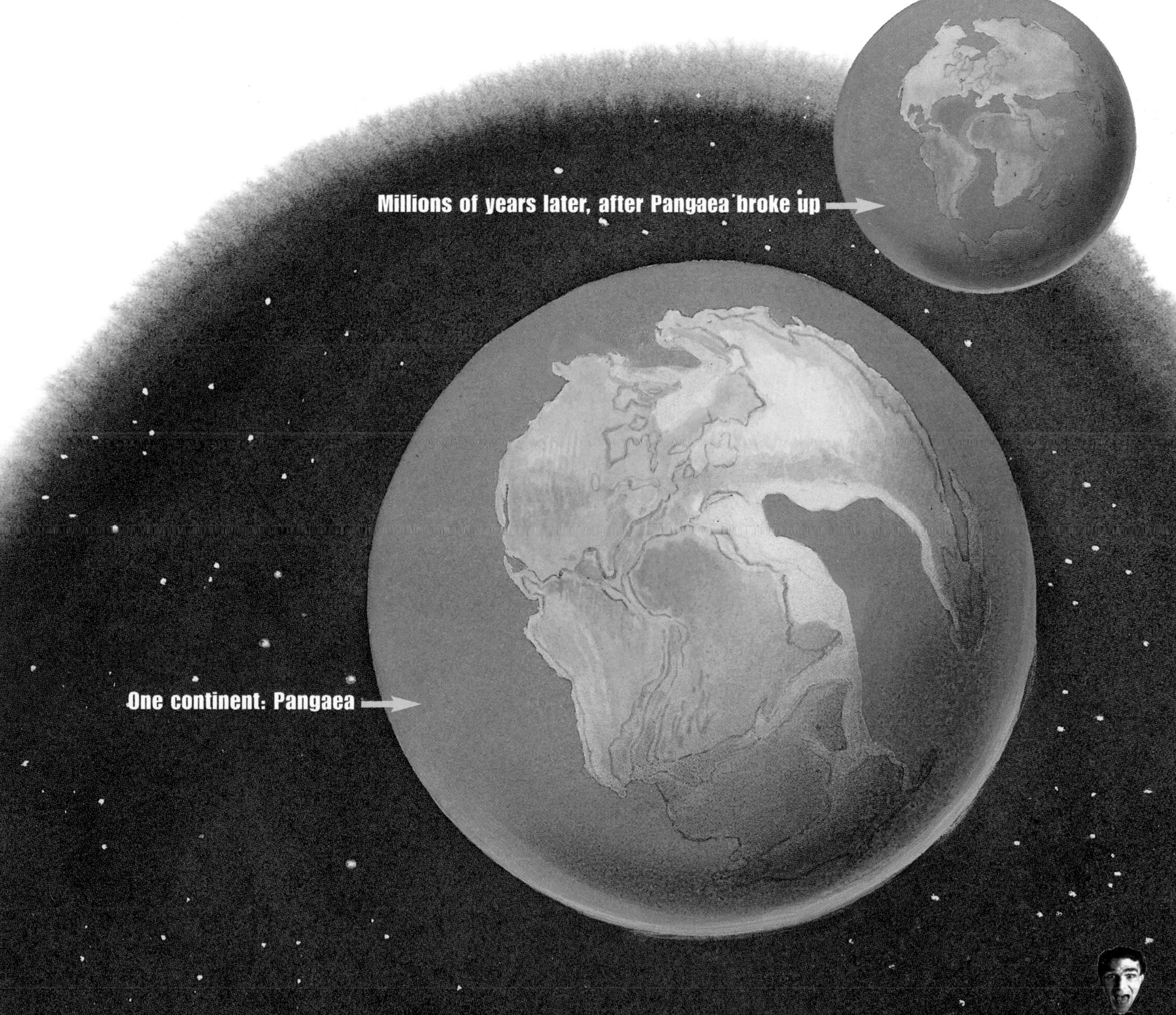

The hot magma that is constantly churning around inside the Earth made Pangaea break apart. It took humans about a million years to figure out that we're walking around on slowly, slowly moving gigantic plates of land. By the way, South America is still moving away from Africa at about 1.2 centimeters (½ inch) a year. That's not too fast, but in a few million years, where do you think your hometown will end up?

Earth still was just one big continent during the Triassic Period. It wasn't until 206–146 million years ago, during the Jurassic Period, that the continents started to spread out.

Try this. You'll have the whole world in your pan.

TRY THIS!

THE QUESTION:

What makes continental plates move?

HERE'S WHAT YOU NEED:

waxed paper • a thin metal pie pan • a microwave oven or teakettle
a coffee mug • a dinner plate • some water • food coloring • an adult

1. Cut two or three continents out of waxed paper in any shape you like—just keep them small, about 3 centimeters (1¼ inches) across.
2. Fill a metal pan with about 1 centimeter (⅜ inch) of cool water. Place your continents on the surface of the water.
3. Ask an adult to help you boil 350 ml (1½ cups) of water.
4. Place the coffee mug in the middle of the plate. Pour the hot water in the mug until it just overflows.
5. Put the pie pan on top of the hot cup. Your continents will be driven to drift apart slowly by the heat under the pan. Put a couple of drops of food coloring near the middle and along the edge.

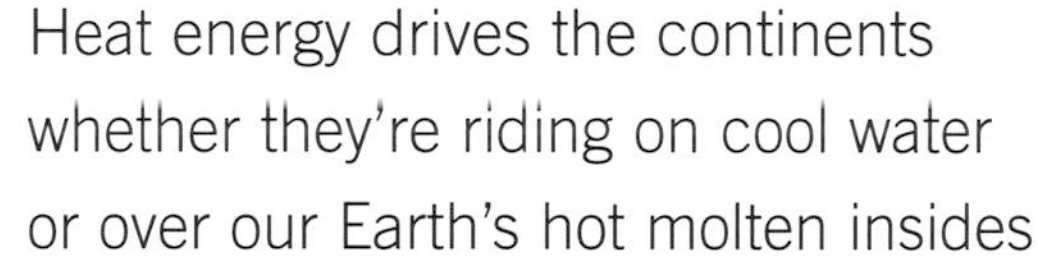

Heat energy drives the continents whether they're riding on cool water or over our Earth's hot molten insides.

Were Dinosaurs LIKE US, or NOT?

Deinonychus [Dye-NAHN-ih-kuss] **wasn't too big, compared to some of his peers, at only five feet tall—but his long, sharp, curved claws made him dangerous.**

In many ways, ancient dinosaurs were nothing like us. Many of them had scaly skin or feathers. Their offspring hatched out of eggs. In other ways, dinosaurs were a lot like us. They breathed air, ran around on land, and hung out with others of their own kind. Also, they must have had ways to communicate, as the birds of today do.

Some ancient dinosaurs, like *Parasaurolophus* [pair-uh-Sorr-uh-LAH-fuss], had huge hollow spaces in their heads. Maybe they were for making trumpeting sounds. That would be like carrying about 10 extra kilograms (20 punds) around on top of their heads just to communicate with one another.

That's two watermelons' worth!

Paleontologists digging in the Patagonian desert of Argentina unearthed a nearly complete dinosaur nesting site. This amazing find revealed not only well-preserved eggs with the remains of dinosaur babies in them but also the imprint of young dinosaur skin.

LIKE US, OR NOT?

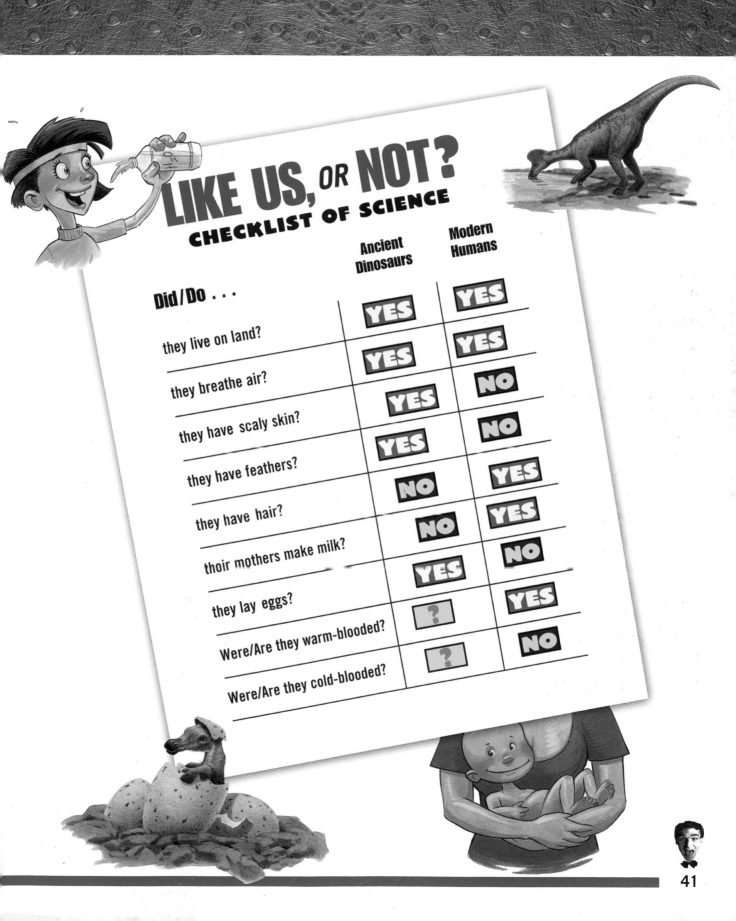

CHECKLIST OF SCIENCE

Did/Do . . .	Ancient Dinosaurs	Modern Humans
they live on land?	YES	YES
they breathe air?	YES	YES
they have scaly skin?	YES	NO
they have feathers?	YES	NO
they have hair?	NO	YES
thoir mothers make milk?	NO	YES
they lay eggs?	YES	NO
Were/Are they warm-blooded?	?	YES
Were/Are they cold-blooded?	?	NO

Some dinosaurs lived in family groups, as we do. Scientists figured this out when they discovered groups of nests full of fossil dinosaur eggs. We can get a good estimate of how big mother and dad dinosaurs were by measuring the distance between their nests. Ancient dinosaurs, like modern birds, must have needed enough room to move around between nests without thwapping neighbor nests with their tails. In general, the distance between nests is about the same as the length of the animal. We learned this by observing modern birds like penguins.

Some modern birds live together in big bird neighborhoods we call rookeries. That's where birds raise their offspring. It looks like some ancient dinosaurs raised their babies the same way.

TRY THIS!

THE QUESTION:

How did dinosaurs communicate?

HERE'S WHAT YOU NEED:

an assortment of plastic soda or water bottles
(try a ½-liter, a 1-liter, and three 2-liter bottles) • scissors • an adult

1. Put your mouth right up to the edge of the ½-liter bottle. Blow gently across the top, the way a flute player makes music. Try it with each bottle.
2. Cut the bottom off one of the 2-liter bottles and the top off the other 2-liter bottle. Tape them together, and you've got a double-long dinosaur head. Try blowing across the top again. The longer the bottle, the lower the sound you'll make.
3. Now try humming through your nose while you blow through your mouth. Make your own dinosaur communication sounds.

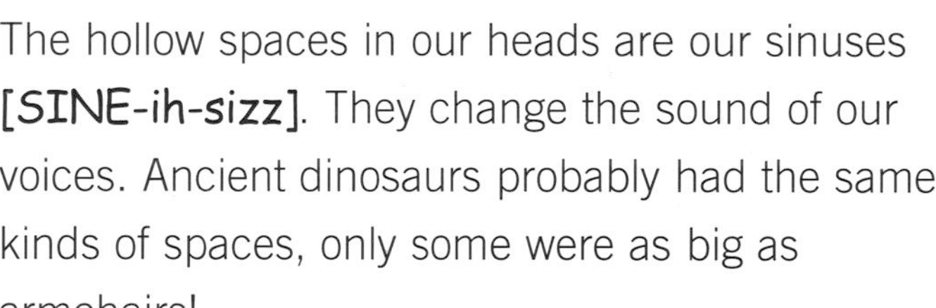

The hollow spaces in our heads are our sinuses [SINE-ih-sizz]. They change the sound of our voices. Ancient dinosaurs probably had the same kinds of spaces, only some were as big as armchairs!

CAMPTOSAURUS

Camptosaurus [Kamp-tuh-SORR-uss] was pretty flexible. He or she could walk on two or four legs, and also had a horned beak.

from ancient DINOSAUR to Bird

Scientists today are pretty sure that birds came from the theropod dinosaurs. They figured this out by comparing the shapes of bones of ancient birds like *Archaeopteryx* [Ar-kee-AHP-ter-iks] with the fossils of ancient theropods like *Velociraptors*. These animals all had S-shaped necks. They walked on two legs with three big toes pointing forward. Their leg bones were set up so that their knees were always bent as they walked.

Some theropods also had fibers or thin plates that stuck out from their skin like the teeth of a comb. Some even had feathers like those of our modern birds.

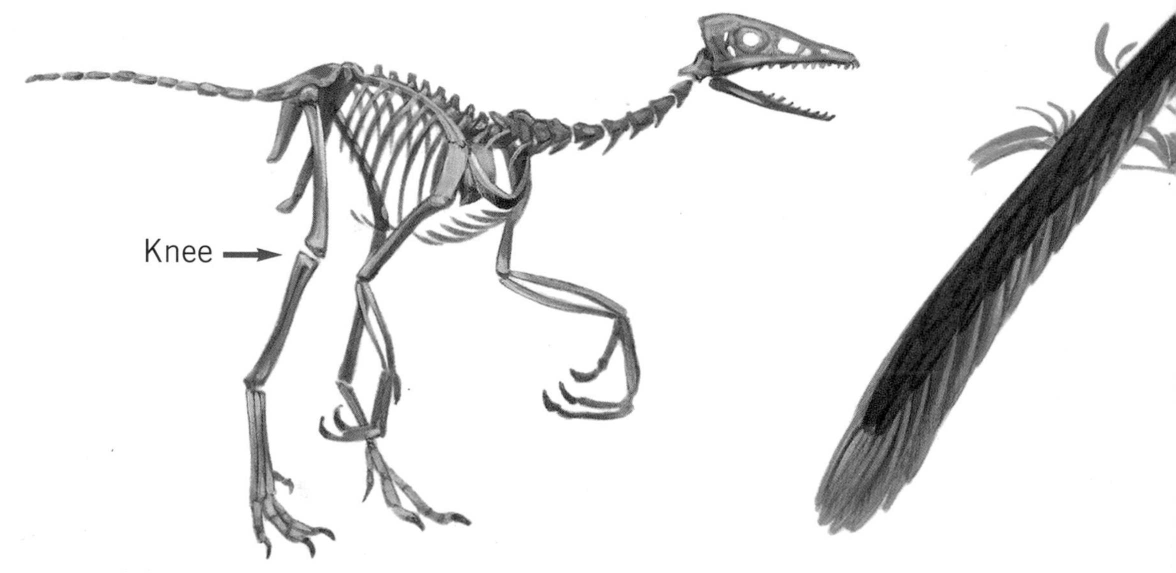

We stand with our knees straight. Well, we're not theropods.

CHECK IT OUT!

Birds that can fly have feathers that are almost straight on the front edge and curved on the back edge, like a kayak paddle. When scientists find feather fossils, they check the edges (if they can find them) to get an idea of whether or not the animal they are investigating could fly.

It Could Be in Their Genes There are still many things about the ancient dinosaurs that we don't know, but maybe there is a way to find out. Your body is made of tiny compartments called cells. Those dinosaurs also had cells (like birds and reptiles). In almost every cell, there are long molecules called deoxyribonucleic acid [dee-Ok-see-RIE-boe-new-KLAY-ik ASS-id], or DNA. The bundles of DNA are what we call our "genes" [jeenz]. DNA molecules are two strands of complex chemicals wrapped together, like a twisted ladder. The twisted shape of each "rail" on the ladder is called a helix [HEE-liks]. Together, the strands are called a double helix. These molecules provide all the information needed to make an animal, plant, or dinosaur. It may be possible to figure out which part of an animal's genes determine whether she or he has a heart that can pump warm blood around.

It's long been thought that if we could get hold of dinosaur DNA, we could know exactly what a dinosaur looked like. Mosquitoes existed during the period dinosaurs were around, and they bit them, just as they bite humans now. Scientists have extracted pieces of DNA from insects trapped in ancient tree sap. But the pieces are still incomplete. There could be other ways to extract dinosaur DNA. Maybe you'll figure one of them out.

TRY THIS!

THE QUESTION:

Just how long is a DNA molecule?

HERE'S WHAT YOU NEED:

two rolls of different colored crepe paper • colored pens
a big room • a globe

1 Roll out both rolls of crepe paper. Using different colored pens, write along the length of each of them a description of all the characteristics that a DNA molecule would tell you about a dinosaur—"really tall, scaly skin, big claws, long tail, carnivore, warm-blooded," etc.

2 Twist your rolls of crepe paper into a double helix.

3 Hang your twisted-paper DNA molecule from one side of a room to the other.

4 DNA is about 500 million times as long as it is wide. Your model would have to stretch 22,000 kilometers (14,000 miles), a little over halfway around the globe!

It takes a lot of genetic information to make an animal like you or a Camptosaurus.

Ancient Dinosaur Index

Allosaurus [AL-uh-Sorr-uss]: "different lizard"
9 meters (20 feet) long, 2.5 tons,
saurischian

Ankylosaurus [ang-KYLE-uh-Sorr-uss]: "armored lizard"
7 meters (23 feet) long, 1.7 tons,
ornithischian

Apatosaurus (formerly Brontosaurus) [Ah-Pah-tuh-SORR-uss]:
"deceptive lizard"
25 meters (80 feet) long, 15 tons,
saurischian

Argentinosaurus [arr-jen-TEEN-uh-Sorr-uss]:
"lizard from Argentina"
40 meters (130 feet) long, 90 tons(!),
saurischian

Brachiosaurus [BRAK-ee-uh-Sorr-uss]: "arm lizard"
26 meters (85 feet) long, 14 meters (45 feet) tall, 50 tons,
saurischian

Camptosaurus [Kamp-tuh-SORR-uss]: "bent lizard"
6 meters (20 feet) long, 1 meter (3 feet) tall, 1.5 tons,
ornithischian

Compsognathus [Komp-sahg-NA-thus]: "pretty jaw"
1 meter (3 feet) long, 3 kilograms (6.5 lbs.),
saurischian

Corythosaurus [kor-Ith-uh-SORR-uss]: "helmet lizard"
9 meters (30 feet) long, 5 tons,
ornithischian

Deinonychus [Die-NAHN-ih-kuss]:"terrible claw"
3 meters (10 feet) long, 1.5 meters (5 feet) tall,
80 kilograms (180 lbs),
saurischian

Diplodocus [Dip-LAH-dik-uss]: "double beamed"
30 meters (100 feet) long, 5 tons,
saurischian

Edmontonosaurus [ed-MUHN-tuh-Sorr-uss]:
"lizard from Edmonton, Canada"
13 meters (60 feet) long, 3.5 tons,
ornithischian

Eoraptor [Ee-oh-RAPP-ter]: "dawn (robber)"
1 meter (3 feet) long, 30 kilograms (70 lbs.),
saurischian

Giganotosaurus [jie-gan-NAH-tuh-Sorr-uss]: "gigantic lizard"
15 meters long, (50 feet), 8 tons,
saurischian

Iguanodon [Ih-GWAN-uh-Dahn]: "iguana toothed"
9 meters (30 feet) long, 5 meters (16 feet) tall, 4.5 tons,
ornithischian

Maiasaura [Mie-uh-Sorr-uh]: "good mother lizard"
9 meters (30 feet) long, 2 meters (6 feet) high, 3 tons,
ornithischian

Megalosauripus [May-gah-luh-Sorr-ih-puss]:
"great lizard foot"
height and weight unknown,
saurischian

Pachycephalosaurus [Pak-ee-SEF-uh-luh-Sorr-uss]:
"thick-headed lizard"
5 meters (16 feet) long, 1 ton,
ornithischian

Parasaurolophus [pair-uh-Sorr-uh-LAH-fuss]:
"beside Saurolophus (crested lizard)"
10 meters long (33 feet), 5 (16 feet) meters tall, 3-4 tons,
ornithischian

Plateosaurus [Platt-ee-uh-SORR-uss]: "flat lizard"
8 meters (26 feet) long, 1.5 tons,
saurischian

Scelidosaurus [SKEL-EYE-duh-SORR-uss]: "limb lizard"
4 meters (13 feet) long, 0.8 tons,
ornithischian

Seismosaurus [SIZE-muh-Sorr-us]:"quake lizard"
45 meters (150 feet) long, 15 tons,
saurischian

Thescelosaurus [THESS-eh-luh-Sorr-uss]: "marvelous lizard"
4 meters (13 feet) long, 0.3 tons,
ornithischian

Titanosaurus [Tie-TAN-uh-Sorr-uss]: "titanic lizard"
15 meters (50 feet) long, (15) tons,
saurischian

Torosaurus [TOR-uh-Sorr-uss]: "bull lizard"
7 meters (23 feet), 7.5 tons
ornithischian

Triceratops [Try-SAIR-uh-tops]:
"three-horned face"
8 meters long (26 feet), 10 tons,
ornithiscian

It sure did take us a long time to get here.

Tyrannosaurus rex [tih-RAN-ih-Sorr-uss]:
"tyrant lizard king"
12 meters (40 feet) long, 5–7 tons,
saurischian

Ultrasaurus [ULL-trah-Sorr-uss]:
"beyond big lizard"
17 meters (56 feet) long, 27 tons,
saurischian

Utahraptor [YEW-taw-Rapp-ter]:
"robber from Utah"
6.5 meters (21 feet), 1 ton,
saurischian

Velociraptor [veh-LAHSS-ih-Rapp-ter]: "speedy thief"
1.7 meters (5.5 feet) long, 1 meter tall,
11 kg (24 lbs),
saurischian

2 million years ago human ancestors appear
0.02 million years ago humans like you